DEAD WEIGHT

Sam Falkirk, Captain in the World Police stationed at the World Council in New York, investigates the death of Angelo Augustine, a Council employee. Superficially a parcel courier, Angelo had also spied for Senator Rayburn, whose power-hungry plan is the destruction of the Orient. Meanwhile, Senator Sucamari of the Japanese legation has a deadly plan himself, involving a parcel containing a Buddha coated with enough bacteria to cause a plague across the Americas. When the parcel is stolen can Falkirk find the criminal in time?

E. C. TUBB

DEAD WEIGHT

Complete and Unabridged

LINFORD
Leicester

First published in Great Britain

First Linford Edition
published 2007

British Library CIP Data

Tubb, E. C.
   Dead weight.—Large print ed.—
Linford mystery library
   1. Detective and mystery stories
   2. Large type books
   I. Title
   823.9′12 [F]

   ISBN 978–1–84617–602–9

Published by
F. A. Thorpe (Publishing)
Anstey, Leicestershire

Set by Words & Graphics Ltd.
Anstey, Leicestershire
Printed and bound in Great Britain by
T. J. International Ltd., Padstow, Cornwall

This book is printed on acid-free paper

1

Trouble at Nations Square

The trouble started in Nations Square. A corner-prophet had climbed the plinth of Blue's statue and was haranguing a small crowd. He was a gaunt man with sunken eyes and a straggling beard. He wore a tattered suit that had once been mauve but was now a dark brown with dirt and wear. Sandals covered his bare feet and his speech was interrupted by bouts of violent coughing. He was about sixty years old and should have had better sense than to stand thinly clad in the open at the beginning of winter. He was also wasting his time.

Sam Falkirk eased his weight from one foot to the other as he stood at the edge of the crowd and listened to the thin, strident voice of the corner-prophet. It was the usual tirade; a plea for the Blues to be allowed civil rights and

1

representation, an attack against society for not permitting them to offer their labour in the open market, and a complaint that, though legally dead, they still had to pay taxes on everything they bought.

Sam had heard it all before and only stayed because he had ten minutes to kill before returning to duty. Behind the statue the soaring bulk of the World Council buildings lifted towards the sky, framing the end of the square and facing on the Hudson. Within the buildings air-conditioning kept the offices at a comfortable temperature, but Sam liked to feel the incipient bite of winter in the fresh air.

Also the speaker amused him. Sam could guess at his exact progress. He would rant and rave, shake his fist and make tremendous demands while all the time the crowd would watch with apathetic contempt. Some might heckle him a little, others might shout personal abuse, but mostly the corner-prophets were tolerated as sort of modern-age clowns. Sam had overlooked the teenagers.

They had joined the crowd so quietly that he wasn't aware of their presence until they started business. There were about twenty of them, all males, all wearing tight black jerseys, tight black pants, thick-soled shoes and long-peaked caps pulled over their eyes. The jerseys were marked front and back with a white, grinning skull. Each of them carried a long walking stick. Sam had seen similar sticks before. They were lead-loaded and could snap a shin or crush a skull as if the bone were made of eggshell.

Sam was no coward, but he knew his limitations. The crowd would be no help; they wouldn't want to get hurt. The corner-prophet, the obvious target for the young hooligans, was surrounded. At best he could expect a beating; at worst he could be killed or so crippled that life would be a torment. And Sam, if he tried anything on his own, would receive the same treatment. Gently he eased himself from the crowd.

The nearest videophone booth was occupied. Sam jerked open the door, pulled out a protesting woman, and shut himself in the booth. He pressed the emergency button, and identified himself as the screen flashed to life.

'Captain Sam Falkirk of the World Police. Emergency call to local police. Trouble due at Nations Square. Blue's statue. Teenagers, about twenty of them, on a Blue-hunt.'

'I'll handle it.' The screen went blank as the operator cut the connection.

Outside the booth the woman was still fuming with outraged dignity. Sam hesitated, about to apologize, then changed his mind as he saw what was happening around the statue. The teenagers had moved in, swinging their sticks against legs and heads to clear a path to where the corner-prophet huddled in helpless terror. Sam reached the plinth just too late. A dozen of the toughs laughed and joked as they poked and prodded at the prophet writhing and screaming on the ground. Sam dodged a stick swinging at his skull, snatched at it and, at the same time, kicked its owner in the stomach. The stick in his hands, he jumped forward to straddle the prostrate man, felt

4

something hit his shoulder and just managed to parry a vicious thrust at his eyes.

The next few seconds were a blur of motion as he lashed desperately at the ring of hooligans. Their clothing was padded and Sam, a grown man, couldn't bring himself to hit full-strength at the youngsters. They had no such compunction. Sam would have been beaten to a pulp but for the arrival of the police.

They came whining up on their crash bikes, over a dozen of them, and at the sound of their approach the teenagers melted away, running lightly for the substrips where they would be safe.

'You hurt?' A burly sergeant, recognising Sam by his uniform, halted by his side.

'No.' Sam examined himself to make sure. 'No, I'm all right. I wouldn't have been though if you hadn't arrived so soon.' He looked to where two officers stooped over the prophet. 'How is he?'

'He'll live.' One of the men straightened. 'Needs hospitalization, though.'

'Send for the ambulance.' The sergeant

returned his attention to Sam. 'Did you recognize any of them?'

'The teenagers?' Sam shook his head. 'Not personally. They all wore skull-markings though; that should help.'

'It won't.' The sergeant was pessimistic. 'I know that bunch; they'll cover each other up no matter what.' He shrugged. 'Well, it's just another of those things. Thanks, anyway, captain. No need for you to hang around if you're busy.'

It was, as the sergeant had said, just another of those things. There was no surprise or horror at the thought of a gang of young hooligans beating a man almost to death for the sheer fun of it. No explanation, either, though the psychologists had tried. They said the Blue-baiting was due to a need for excitement, a desire on the part of the youngsters to assert themselves or a breaking through of the primitive. For private consumption they had a different reason. They said that it was due to a conditioned hatred of all Blues and anything appertaining to them. It was, they said, a natural revolt of youth against age.

Which didn't really account for the teenagers having chosen the corner-prophet as a victim, though, with his white hair and beard and unhealthy pallor he could have passed for a Blue. None of them, apparently, had bothered to check for the star he should have had tattooed on the back of his left hand.

* * *

A man was waiting for Sam as he entered the vestibule. He was a plump man, wearing a suit of lime green edged with white piping. His face was round and smooth but his hair was touched with grey and the skin beneath his eyes was soft and flaccid. He carried a briefcase in one hand. He stepped forward with an ingratiating smile.

'Captain Falkirk?'

'Yes?'

'I'd like to speak with you for a moment if I may.' He produced a card. 'Frank Perbright, Acme Insurance.'

'Not interested.' Sam brushed past the man and headed for the elevators.

Perbright, not to be dissuaded, scurried at his side.

'Please, captain, this is important.' He looked at the humming activity all around them. 'If we could go somewhere quiet? Your office, perhaps?'

'Is this official business?' Sam stared at the plump man. 'If it is, you'd better come up to my office. If it isn't, then we can speak down here. Well?'

'It isn't official business,' admitted Perbright. He didn't sound happy about it. 'But it is important.'

'To whom?' Sam felt that he could guess the answer but he didn't feel like arguing. He led the way to a lecture room, peeped inside and gestured to Perbright. The room was occupied by a visiting class of schoolchildren and the lecturer was telling them about the greatest discovery of all time. He was a good speaker, his words clear and distinct, and his command of the students was absolute. He was a good instructor. He was a hundred and twenty years old.

'Doctor Edward Henry Clarence Blue discovered his serum ninety-five years ago now, back in 2016. The serum is a combination of radioactive isotopes, which in some way, wash the body free of age-poisons and arrest the advance of old age. It does more than that. It partially restores youth, in that it allows the body to rebuild itself without hindrance from those poisons. An old man will grow more youthful. His arteries will regain their elasticity, his joints lose their accumulations of uric deposits and his bones become less brittle. And, for some reason, he will also be proof against disease. He will, in effect, be immortal.'

Sam edged his way into the room as the instructor paused, Perbright following him. They sat down at the back of the lecture room. The instructor glanced towards them, then resumed his discourse.

'Just why that should be so no one quite knows. No one knows why, by some freak action of the serum, all melanin is bleached from the body so that Blues, as those who take the treatment are popularly called, are always albinos.' The instructor lifted his left hand and showed the star tattooed on the back, above the fingers. 'The second identifying mark is this star.' He didn't, Sam noticed, explain the purpose of the star. Many Blues had tried to disguise themselves with make-up and dye and so take and hold jobs normally reserved for non-Blues. The compulsory tattoo was a way of preventing such deception. He turned as Perbright called to him.

'Captain Falkirk.'

'What is it?'

'Just this,' the plump man drew coloured folders from his briefcase, 'captain. I'd like to explain the details of our new policy. I feel that it is one of the most beneficial ever offered to the public, and is of special interest to those in your position . . . '

'I thought you said that this was important,' interrupted Sam irritably. 'I'm already insured.'

'But only against sickness and the cost of treatment when it becomes necessary,' said Perbright quickly. 'But what of the future, captain? Have you ever thought of that?' He riffled the folders. 'Now, for just one fifth of your income during the term of your natural life we guarantee to provide you with Restezee facilities after you have taken the treatment.'

'Not interested,' said Sam curtly.

'But, captain!' Perbright sounded desperate. 'You just can't afford not to be interested. 'Let me point out that . . . '

Sam sat back, relaxing and letting the plump man's words pass over his head. He wasn't interested in insurance, though, apparently, the insurance companies were in him. They were probably still trying to recoup the money they had lost in paying out annuities and pensions long after they had expected. When Blue had announced his discovery they had been the ones to immediately suffer. Life policies and endowments had stopped and everyone had turned to annuities. The tardy legislation that had legally killed all Blues had been engineered by the insurance companies as a matter of sheer self defence. Something Perbright said attracted his attention.

'Now, wait a minute,' said Sam. 'This doesn't make sense. You say that for one fifth of my income I'll be taken care of for long as I want. Right?'

'That's perfectly right, captain.'

'Well, how can you do it? Even if I manage to last another thirty years that still only enables you to keep me for six at my accustomed standard. What's the catch?'

'No catch, captain.' Perbright became more persuasive. 'Naturally, you will be expected to help out by doing some work, but that's to be expected.'

'Is it?' Sam was thoughtful. 'I think that I'd better have the department look into this. If your company is thinking of starting a Blue sweat-shop it had better be investigated.'

'It's legal,' protested Perbright.

'And what can you lose? The way things are you've got no future. You're unmarried, without children and all on your own.'

'That's enough.' Sam was annoyed. 'I don't like being investigated by cheap-skate operators. You'd better go before I have you thrown out.'

'I'm going.' Perbright grabbed at his

briefcase. 'But think it over, captain. If you want me you can find me in the book.'

Alone, Sam sat and tried to control his anger. He didn't like being taken for a fool, and Perbright had pulled something too raw to stomach. That part about children, for example.

Sam blinked as he heard his name. The instructor, smiling from where he stood on the dais, beckoned to him.

'Now for a few words from Captain Falkirk of the World Police. I want you to pay great attention to what he has to say. Captain Falkirk.'

Sam rose, feeling a little foolish beneath the steady stare of sixty pairs of eyes. It wouldn't have been so bad had he been a heroic character, someone over six feet tall, say, with wide shoulders and the profile of a tv star. But he was just an ordinary, quiet-seeming man with brown hair and brown eyes and a sensitive mouth. His figure, thanks to gymnastics, was good, and he had a certain appeal to women. A cheeky-faced tot winked at him as he climbed the dais and he felt a lot better.

He knew, too, what he was expected to say; he had done this at odd times before. He rested his hands on the table in unconscious imitation of the instructor, leaned a little towards the microphone and came straight to the point.

'You have heard your instructor tell you something of the past and how it has affected the present. You may be wondering what I have to say to you. The answer is this. I want to remind you that we all live in one world, that we are one people and that the youth of today is the old person of tomorrow.'

He paused, staring at them, wondering what impression he was making. Probably none; children have short memories.

'Soon you will be teenagers,' he continued. 'You may have heard some of the things which teenagers are supposed to do. Some of them actually do such things, but it isn't funny or clever to do them. It isn't funny to go on a Blue-bait, it isn't clever to gang up against a man old enough to be your great-great-great-grandfather, it isn't amusing to deride old people for being old. Most of you have

Blues living at home. You may have heard your parents, at times, talking about them as if they were a nuisance. Some of you may even feel that life would be much easier if they weren't around. That is the wrong attitude.'

Wrong, but who could blame them? Unless they had special qualifications, Blues were in a bad way. Some were protected by the government, a few scientists and others of value, but the great majority, able to find only casual work, were mostly objects of charity. Work was found for them when possible, but no Blue could be legally or morally employed while a non-Blue needed work.

For the young had their own lives to live, families to raise and relations to support. Each new generation had the task of helping to support those who had gone before. A man now raised a large family so that, when he took the treatment, the children he had raised could support him. Some did, others didn't. Some meekly bore the filial yoke, while others cut free from responsibility and started out fresh on their own. No one could blame them; they committed no crime, but unsupported Blues, crippled by their lack of legal rights, became pitiful objects.

It was better for society if the Family bond remained strong. But the young, at times, are thoughtlessly cruel. At all times they are impatient.

'Be kind,' ended Sam. 'Be patient. Be understanding. At all times remember that, one day, you, too, will be a Blue. Always think of that when you are with them. What they are, you will be. Treat them as such.'

The instructor dismissed the class then and thanked Sam for his trouble. 'Part of my job,' Sam remembered the incident by the statue. 'If we can persuade one of those children to refrain from joining in a Blue-bait, then no trouble is too much. If we can instil in them the concept that all Blues are just as human and just as normal as they are, then any amount of trouble is justified. The time to prevent crime is during the formative years. Punishing them later is an admission that our educational techniques are at fault.'

'I agree.' Absently the instructor rubbed the back of his left hand. 'If we had full control of the children for the first fifteen years of their lives we could build a model society.' He shrugged. 'The usual lament. We teach them one thing and their parents, by example, teach them another.' He became thoughtful. 'You mentioned Blue-baiting. Is it bad?'

'It's getting worse, and it's not only confined to teenagers. There have been reports of lynch-mobs at work.' Sam looked grim. 'It's the same principle, though they aren't composed of teenagers. Many against one and God help the individual.'

'And the individual is always a Blue.' The instructor shuddered. 'Horrible! To think that men could do such things!'

'They do them.' Sam glanced at his watch. 'I'm late. You'll pardon me?'

'Of course.' The instructor held out his hand. 'And thank you again for your trouble.'

'It was no trouble,' said Sam. 'I like kids.' It was true, too. Perhaps not in the mass, but he would have liked a couple of his own. A boy, say, like the one who had winked at him, and a girl like the one with the pigtails and the candy-striped frock.

Outside in the vestibule Sam paused to stare through the doors to where the statue of Blue dominated the square. The late October sunshine shone on the polished granite and a few pigeons fluttered over the sidewalks on their eternal search for crumbs. Everything looked very peaceful.

Sam didn't know that trouble was heading towards him at twenty-five hundred miles an hour.

2

Senator Rayburn

Two years earlier, on the island of Hainan, south of the province of Kwang-Tung, the first soil had been turned for the construction of a big new Chorella plant now completed and ready for operation. It was a World Council project, naturally; no one else had either the money or the inclination to spend billions of dollars in order to provide a source of cheap, nutritious food for the Orient.

Senator Sucamari conducted the opening ceremony, his clipped Cantonese matching his yellow skin and slanted eyes, his face impassive as he pressed the button that started the primary pumps. Senator Rayburn represented the Occident, but where Rayburn concentrated on smiling into the newsfax cameras that transmitted the scene all over the world, the Japanese knew better. Instead, he terminated the ceremony with a short speech emphasizing the dire need of many more such installations, praised various ancestors and managed, without apparent effort or intention, to make the American appear an ill-mannered schoolboy.

Rayburn was glad when it was all over.

★ ★ ★

From Hainan to New York was a four-hour flight in the big stratoliner, soaring high above the atmosphere in an elliptical curve that would terminate in the Hudson. From there to the World Council buildings on Manhattan would take another hour.

Rayburn didn't like the journey. Air transport was as safe as could be devised, but there was always the element of risk. He stared down through the window by his seat at the earth below, showing a distinct curvature at this height, and tried to rid himself of the thought of what would happen should anything go wrong. Probably nothing but a little discomfort.

The pressurized cabin could be detached from the main structure and would parachute down to safety. It was buoyant, fitted with shock absorbers and contained its own radio-sending equipment, together with emergency rations and crash gear. The worst that could happen was that the passengers would have to wait for rescue.

But it was a long, long way down. And the tanks behind the cabin were awash with highly explosive. And perhaps, if anything did happen, the parachutes wouldn't open, and they would go falling, falling, falling . . . Rayburn shook is head to rid himself of morbid thoughts and stared about the cabin.

Across the aisle Nagati sat reading, a fat, diplomatic bag resting between his feet. Ahead of his aide, Sucamari, seemingly relaxed, stared at something invisible before him. Rayburn didn't like the Japanese; he was too calm, too bland, too polite. It was impossible to tell what went on inside that small, round head, behind that emotionless, eternal smile. Sucamari was always smiling, except when, as now, he stared at something other men couldn't see. His own thoughts Rayburn imagined; sometimes he did the same thing himself. The Japanese suddenly turned, his smile flicking on as he met Rayburn's stare.

'Nice opening,' said Rayburn. He was never put out by the unexpected.

'It gave joy to many,' said Sucamari. He spoke better English than the American, and his Cantonese had been equal to that of a native. Rumour had it that he spent long hours with a hypno-tutor in order to perfect his linguistic ability. Rayburn didn't know about that, and he didn't care. He himself only spoke one language, his own, and left the interpreters to worry about the translations.

'It may have given joy to those on the receiving end,' he said pointedly. 'But I'm not so sure about the rest.'

'Is charity, then, a lost virtue?'

'Charity begins at home.'

'Home?' Sucamari's smile didn't alter.

'You know what I mean,' snapped Rayburn. 'The World Council levies a toll on each country according to its productivity and natural wealth. The Americas pay more than anyone else. We've our own troubles, too, you know, and we can't be expected to keep paying out vast sums for the benefit of backward peoples.'

'Backward?' Sucamari's smile became a little strained. 'May I remind you that the Orient contains cultures which were old before the Americas were discovered? I would not call them backward.'

'That is your opinion.' Rayburn held out his left hand. Despite the insecticides with which the plant-area had been saturated, the flies had been a nuisance. He pointed to the bites. 'Is this an example of progress? Disease-carriers allowed to breed unchecked on deliberately exposed filth?' He was referring to the habit of the natives in using natural waste products to fertilize their land instead of washing it down into sewers for scientific processing.

'Old habits die hard,' said Sucamari quietly. 'And what else can they do? The soil is poor, worked out, and the supply of phosphates and artificial fertilizers scarce. They merely do as their ancestors did before them.'

'Ancestors!' Rayburn was about to say more when caution dictated silence. Sucamari was an Oriental, educated in the Occident though he might be. Ancestor worship was a part of his culture, and to speak against it would be to attack his religious beliefs. 'At least,' he said mildly, 'they could try harder to exterminate the pests.'

'They could, but they won't,' agreed Sucamari. 'Most of them are Buddhists and, to them, all life is sacred, even that of the lowliest insects. There have been unpleasant incidents at the sites of the spray-aircraft and others when extermination teams have tried to wipe out unwanted carnivores and other low-life forms.' He shrugged. 'Foolish, perhaps, but there it is.'

'Foolish is right,' said Rayburn. 'As I understand it the Buddhists believe in reincarnation of the soul into animals and other creatures. Well, now that there is no natural death they don't have to worry about reincarnation, do they? So why cling to the old beliefs?'

'Your logic is at fault; that, or your

understanding of Buddhism.' Sucamari was very patient. 'People still die, you know, and infant mortality in the Orient is quite high. Also, no matter how many people are alive now, they cannot be more than all the people who have lived before them. So, to a Buddhist, there are still a number of souls awaiting rebirth in human form.'

'Foolishness,' repeated Rayburn. 'Dangerous foolishness at that. With their unsanitary conditions they are begging for trouble in allowing vermin to exist as they do.'

'Perhaps, but what can we do? Religious freedom must be respected or there can be no freedom.'

It was defeat, as it was always defeat, when he argued with the Japanese. Rayburn slumped back into his seat and stared moodily through the window. Words, always words, and yet words had their uses as he well knew. He could whip an audience into a frenzy with carefully chosen phrases which touched off predictable responses but, when it came to the test, what were words? Only a means to gain control of force, the final argument against which words were useless.

And the final argument was coming.

Rayburn remembered the long, patient lines of coolies back in Hainan. The dense woods which had once covered the island had long since been cleared away so as to make room for tiny farms, little patches of dirt from which the natives tried to scratch a living. But while the productivity of the soil was limited, that of the natives was not.

They bred because they had to breed. They mated and produced children so as to gain more labour to work the worn-out soil, then had to repeat the cycle again and again. And everything was against them — their religion, which forbade the killing of the very lice that sucked their blood and, worst of all, the ancestor worship that had suddenly acquired a new meaning.

Ancestors, in the old days, had done little harm. They had stifled progress, true, but they had also maintained a culture. The living had burned paper symbols of money and food so as to provide for them in the afterworld; symbols which had cost but a fraction of the things they represented. But living ancestors could not be fed on paper loaves or live in paper houses. Legal death, in the Orient, was ignored; the elders were too highly respected for that. So families beggared themselves to support their living ancestors on a steadily declining subsistence level.

But for how long would they be content with that?

Rayburn sighed, glanced towards Sucamari and then looked away. Still that eternal smile, even when engrossed in his thoughts. It was a mask, Rayburn knew, and a scrap of poorly-remembered prose came to him learned long ago. '*I can smile, and murder as I smile*' — Shakespeare? Possibly the old playwright had known more about human nature than most people gave him credit for, and it was the sort of thing he would have written. Gerald would know if he took the trouble to ask, but his aide was asleep, lying back with closed eyes, his parted lips making him look more of a fool than when awake.

He himself couldn't act as Sucamari did. Not for him the bland, emotionless smile, the iron mask of a facial grimace. Rayburn settled deeper in his seat toying with the scrap of prose, turning and twisting it until it fitted: '*I can make others smile, and murder them as they smile.*' That was himself, the loud-mouthed extrovert who blustered and stormed and was transparently obvious as to arouse no question as to his motives. A self-seeker, a power-mad, would-be dictator, a local farm boy with mud on his boots and dirt in his mouth. He had been called all that and more during his political rise to the Senate of the World Council. He was still called it and, in part, it was true. But only in part.

The entire truth was known only to himself.

A stewardess came down the aisle, a tall, well-formed negress, trim in her uniform of green and grey. She halted by his side. 'Coffee, sir?'

'I think so.' Rayburn stared through the

window. It may have been imagination, but it seemed to him that the earth had lost some of its curvature; He said so, and the stewardess nodded.

'We are on the descent,' she explained. 'We should land in about an hour. Black or white, sir?'

'White, and with plenty of sugar.' Idly he watched the woman take the rest of the orders, pleased that she had asked him first. It was a little thing, but powers built on little things. He called out as she approached his aide. 'He'll take the same as myself.'

'Yes, sir.' She disappeared into the galley.

Gerald Waterman yawned and opened his eyes. He hadn't been asleep, despite appearances; he had long since learned that a man asleep is a man ignored. He liked being ignored. He also liked watching people when they thought they were unobserved. He yawned again and sat upright as the stewardess returned with the coffee.

'Thank you, miss.' He smiled as he accepted his cup. 'When do we land?'

'In about an hour, sir.'

'Thank you.' Gerald knew quite well when they would land he had asked only to impress on the others the fact that he had been asleep when Rayburn had asked the same thing. He sipped his coffee and stared out of the window at his side. 'Did any of you see it?'

'See what?' Rayburn was abrupt.

'Murphy's rocket. I've heard that sometimes, at this height you can see it if you look at just the right place at the right time.'

'I doubt it.' Nagati looked up from his book with a faint air of superiority. 'Murphy's rocket went into an elliptical orbit at four planetary diameters when his engine exploded. It wasn't a very large ship and would be impossible to see unless the sun happened to reflect off the hull at exactly the right angle. Even then,' he added, 'You would probably take it for a satellite of some kind.'

'That's what I said.' Gerald craned his neck as he stared through the window. 'You've got to be in the right place at the right time.'

'Murphy was a fool,' said Rayburn. 'His flight was a waste of time and money. God alone knows what he was trying to prove.'

'He was testing a new engine,' said Gerald quietly. 'He hoped that it would be possible to travel interstellar space.'

'He was looking for new worlds,' said Nagati. 'He hoped to find them in the Alpha Centauri system.'

'Rubbish!'

'Not so.' Nagati was insistent. 'The Lunar Observatory has discovered there are planets in the Alpha system. Some of them with an atmosphere apparently much like our own. Certainly man cannot live on the planets of this system. If he is to find new worlds then they must orbit another star. Murphy hoped to find them.'

'He was still a fool,' snapped Rayburn. 'If we couldn't do it way back in the time of NASA then how could he? Sure, he managed to get hold of an obsolete hull and somehow got the money to fit it up but if his engine was so good why didn't the Council take over?'

'This was before the days of World Government,' explained Nagati patiently.

'That long ago?' Rayburn shrugged. 'That explains it. The guy was a nut. He had to go it alone because he had no option. His engine must have been a load of junk.'

'Prosper didn't think so,' reminded Gerald. 'He used an adaptation of it in his own ship.' He paused. 'And it worked. As far as we know it's still working.'

'Sure,' said Rayburn dismissing the subject. 'As far as we know.'

Gerald didn't argue. Even now, after five years with the senator, he didn't really know whether he admired the man or not. Rayburn was an enigma.

Sometimes he was the shouting loud-mouth, full of wind and devoid of apparent sense, at others he was shrewd and calculating with a computer for a brain and a stone for a heart.

Gerald both admired him for having climbed to power, and despised him for the use he made of it.

Nationalism had died on a day, ninety years ago, when the World Council had drawn the teeth of the warring nations, but Rayburn wouldn't accept that. Instead of working for the new Cosmopolitanism, the creed of brotherly love and mutual aid, he clung stubbornly to old-fashioned ideas of patriotism and restricted loyalties.

If it hadn't been so ludicrous it would have been pathetic, his slinging to the concept that, because a man happened to have been born in a certain locality, he should revere it above all others. As ludicrous as the idea that, because of accident of birth, a man should regard the colour of his skin and the language he spoke as being superior to all others. To Cosmopolitans it was obvious that the world belonged to all men everywhere and could not, and should not, be split into tiny regions. They dreamed of the lay when the final vestiges of nationalism would be swept away, the old boundaries forgotten and all men united into a composite whole. The alternative, as had so often been demonstrated in the past, led only to war.

And war was something no sane man

could contemplate without shuddering revulsion. For people died in time of war, and with modern methods of destruction no one could tell just who would be the victims.

And no one wanted to die and so lose immortality.

Rayburn least of all.

He sat in his seat, his big hands gripping the arm rests, his square, solid, farm-worker's face set in an ugly assortment of crags and hollows. He was sweating, little streams of perspiration trickling from his thin, long white hair. Irritably he mopped his face and neck, annoyed with himself for his weakness.

He was sixty-five years of age and had lived a hard life. He had burned himself out in his drive for power, and the electro-cardiograms showed that his heart was no longer the efficient machine of old. Life, normal life, was running out and the other sort of life, that granted by the serum, would be lost if he waited too long. The treatment had to be taken before the body was too weak and even then it was a gamble. Two percent of those taking it failed to survive, but that was a normal gamble. What wasn't a gamble was the cold certainty that, if he took the treatment, his power would vanish as if it were a dream.

And there was so much to do before he lost that hard-won power.

'Damn it,' Rayburn snapped, squinting through the window. 'Are you sure that we're on time?'

'Is something distressing you, Senator?' Nagati was eager to help. Rayburn waved him aside.

'I'm all right,' he said peevishly. 'It's just that — hell, never mind. You get back to your book.' It was an order he had no right to give and Nagati had no obligation to obey. He hesitated, his face like stone.

'What are you reading?' Sucamari came to the rescue. 'Biology?'

'No, sir. I am studying the equations governing the theory of the Portal. Prosper's Portal. As I understand it the basic premise is that every spot in the universe is identical to every other spot. Therefore movement, motion between two places, is a matter of adjustment rather than actual traversing the distance to be covered. It is rather as if I could penetrate the page of a book instead of having to travel all the way to the edge and back down the other side. I find the concept most intriguing.'

'I am glad of that,' said Sucamari. 'Perhaps you would now care to resume your studies?' He sat back smiling blandly at his fellow senator.

A thin whining began to penetrate the cabin, then relaxed as the stewardess, busy collecting the empty coffee cups, called the usual warning.

'Fasten your safety belts, please. We are about to enter the lower atmosphere.'

Rayburn's hands felt like wood as he fumbled with the straps, his fingers stiff on the buckles. Across the aisle Nagati closed his book, adjusted his straps and touched the diplomatic bag between his feet before settling back against the cushions. Rayburn glanced at Sucamari, then looked up, half in anger, as Gerald, with smooth efficiency, fastened the webbing over chest and thighs. He swallowed the anger; the young fool was only trying to be helpful, but he wished that he didn't feel so old.

He fought the concept, annoyed with himself for yielding to it. He was tired, yes. It had been a long double-journey and the tropical sun had sapped his vigour, but not old. He couldn't be old. There was still too much to do. The plane tilted a little and the whining rose to a shrill scream of displaced air as the stratoliner dropped towards the city below.

3

The statue

Angelo Augustine was a local courier employed by the World Council. Every morning he rose, washed, dressed, kissed his wife, ate a small meal, said goodbye to his dependants and joined the mad rush on the moving ways. For eight hours he worked at his job, which, despite the grandiose title, was little more than being a general messenger and glorified errand boy. Every evening he battled his way home, kissed his wife, ate another small meal and then spent the evening quietly watching television.

Sometimes he altered the routine in that, instead of watching television, he went to the nearby tri-di theatre, sometimes alone, but usually with his wife, Clarissa. At other times he amused himself by making tiny wooden models of sailing ships and, at others, he shut himself away in his study. At such times he said that he was writing a book.

He had followed the same routine for forty years. A small, patient, ordinary-seeming man who obeyed the fifth commandment religiously, paid his insurance and appeared all that he was supposed to be. Appearances can be deceptive. His family would have been surprised to learn that he had a highly efficient knowledge of Oriental languages, a knowledge expensively acquired by hypnotic tuition. They would have been shocked to learn that he had the habit of reading supposedly confidential documents and that, at irregular times, he posted reports of his activities to a box number somewhere on the East Side.

Angelo Augustine was a very efficient spy.

Messengers at the Council building waited in a comfortable room for any demands on their services. There weren't many of them, and all had been checked, counterchecked, tried and tested for utter loyalty and discretion. The World Council was not a single government but a collection of governments, each nation or area sending its own representatives, some of whom lived in the official quarters provided, the majority preferring to reside in their own consulates or private houses.

Communications between nations and representatives, or senators and members of their staff, did not go through normal channels. The diplomatic bag, the courier, the special messenger and the uniformed errand boy still had their place in the scheme of things.

A voice echoed from a speaker and the three messengers waiting in the room listened to instructions.

'Messenger for the French legation. Messenger for the German legation.'

Angelo relaxed as the two other men rose, brushed themselves down and left the room. Five minutes passed. A young man entered, lit a cigarette and sat down with a glossy magazine. He remembered something, rose, crossed the room and pressed a button beneath the speaker.

'Baylis reporting,' he said. 'Available for duty.' He released the button and returned to his chair. He looked at Angelo, who didn't offer to start a conversation, then buried himself in his magazine. Ten minutes later the speaker came to life.

'Messenger for the Australian legation,' said the controller; then, as Angelo rose and headed towards the door. 'Messenger for the Japanese legation.'

'Hell.' Baylis dropped his magazine. 'My luck!' He looked hopefully at the older man. 'How about swapping, Angelo?' he said hopefully. 'I'll do the Aussie and you take the Nip.'

'No,' said Angelo. A good spy is never too eager.

'Why not?' said Baylis. He became confidential. 'Look, there's a girl in the Japanese legation I don't want to see. You know how it is.' He was both good looking and conceited, and his feminine conquests had done nothing to diminish his self-opinion. He caught at Angelo's arm. 'Do me a favour, pal,' he urged. 'Make the swap and help me out. Hell, what difference does it make, anyway?'

'All right,' said Angelo indifferently. A good spy is never too backward. And

41

Baylis was right in what he said, it made no real difference which messenger did what.

The Japanese legation was on the ninety-eighth floor. Angelo waited for the elevator, mounted walked down a carpeted corridor to an office marked with the national emblem of Japan. He knocked, waited, knocked again and entered the office. It was empty.

A good spy never acts out of character. It was in character for a messenger to enter an empty office. It was even in character though not wise if he wanted to retain his job, for him to be a little curious. It was not in character for him to read the documents scattered over the desk, rifle the waste-paper basket or to peer into the filing cabinets. Angelo did none of these things He merely waited, patiently, in the centre of the room.

The girl who joined him a few minutes later was both beautiful and worried. Her high cheekbones and almond eyes were accentuated by her Occidental clothing. She stared at Angelo, registering her disappointment.

'You sent for a messenger, madam?' Angelo, though he was curious, did not betray his curiosity. It was obvious that the girl had hoped to see someone else. It was equally obvious that that someone else was the handsome Baylis.

'Messenger?' The girl blinked, then recovered. 'Yes, of course.' She stared around the office in search of something to justify her summons. Had the messenger been Baylis there would have been no need for such camouflage; they would have been too busy talking. To summon Baylis by name was something that, at the moment, she dared not do. The World Council building was a gigantic sounding board for rumour and scandal, and if the truth were to come out the young man would lose his job. With the labour situation as it was that would be a tragedy. She had every intention of forcing Baylis to marry her, but an unemployed husband is also a bad father. She had to get rid of Angelo and summon another messenger, and then another until Baylis answered the summons. But how to get rid of the old man?

43

'I have a parcel I want you to deliver for me,' she said quickly. She opened a drawer in the desk and took out the package. It was a large, square box and was heavily wrapped in tough, waterproof plastic. It bore no label or address. 'You will deliver it to the Asian antique shop on Park Avenue, New Jersey. That is all.'

'Yes, madam.' Angelo picked up the parcel, a little surprised at its weight, and left the office. He checked out of the building and was heading towards the 42nd Street substrip terminal when he bumped into Sam Falkirk. The captain nodded towards the parcel.

'Hello, Angelo, shopping?'

'Just a delivery job.' Angelo adjusted the parcel beneath his arm. 'Carmen was asking after you, Sam. When can we expect you around at the house?' Carmen was Angelo's daughter, a market research worker who sometimes called at the statistical department of the World Council, and the messenger had secret hopes of Sam becoming his son-in-law.

'As soon as I get some time to call my own,' said Sam. 'Just at the moment, what with school lecture duties and making sure that none of the visitors run off with the fittings or try to smuggle bombs into the assembly chamber, I'm pretty busy.'

'Bombs?'

'That's what I said. Ever since Rayburn got back from Hainan he's been beating the nationalist drum for all it's worth. One day some fanatical Cosmopolitan is going to try and shut him up the hard way.' Sam grinned, but his eyes were serious. Assassination was, as always, a very real danger to those in the public eye.

'Maybe it would be a good idea at that,' said Angelo thoughtfully. 'I've listened to Rayburn and sometimes he gives me the creeps. The trouble is a lot of people believe in him and won't hear a word against him.' He adjusted the parcel again. 'Well, I'd better get on with the job. Any message?'

'For Carmen?' Sam shrugged. 'I don't think so. Just give her my regards and tell her that I'll be calling for a date as soon as I get time,'

Angelo nodded and walked towards the

terminal. As usual, it was crowded, the underground moving ways jammed with an almost solid mass of bodies. Angelo dropped his coin in the turnstile, walked down the ramp to the stationary strip and, holding the parcel in both hands, waited for a clear spot on the five-mile eastbound strip. He saw one, jumped onto the flexible belt and shoved his way across to the next, five miles an hour faster. Again he made the change and leaned on the safety rail as the strip carried him eastwards at fifteen miles an hour.

The strips were uncomfortable but they had partly solved the problem of inter-city transportation. Only partly; nothing could ever wholly solve the continual movement of twenty million people crammed into an area only designed for a third of that number. A hundred years ago the problem had been acute, and since then had grown steadily worse. The substrips had done more than anything else to ease it. They weren't too fast, but they were continuous, and they had been built at a time when a man could literally walk through the city faster than he could drive through the jammed streets.

Angelo closed his eyes as he felt the dampness of artificial mist. It was the cloudscreen of a flashad and his defence was automatic. Not that it did much good; any surface served as a screen for the sub-threshold commands. He opened his eyes as a sexy female voice whispered in his ear. 'Buy Snapbread,' it urged. 'Buy Snapbread. Buy Snapbread.'

The voice faded as he passed out of range. Other speakers would repeat the same message in a strong masculine voice so as to appeal to both sections of the public. Angelo, like most travellers exposed to the nuisance, had developed a high sales resistance to the whisper-speakers, but he could never be quite sure 'that, in consciously not buying Snapbread, he was doing just what the advertiser wanted. Many irritant ads were put out by competing firms for rival products on the theory that what one didn't sell the other would.

The only real defence against advertising was for a man to be both blind and deaf.

Warning lights told of the approach of a junction and Angelo crossed the strips, changing to the one that led under the Hudson. It dipped, leveled, then rose again as it reached the New Jersey shore.

There, Angelo left it. His excuse, had he been observed, was innocent enough. He went to a men's room, fed coins into a slot and closed himself in a cubicle. Alone and safe from observation he got to work.

The outer wrapping of the parcel was a common heat-sealing plastic and it yielded to the urgings of a thin-bladed knife. Inside was a strong corrugated container lined with floss and holding a carved and ornamented box of ivory inlaid with mother of pearl. Angelo removed it, his fingers searching the surface for some means to open it. A spring yielded beneath his thumb and the lid sprang open. Inside the box, nested in more floss, rested a dull brown statue.

It was a statue of Buddha, about eight inches high, six wide and three thick. It was elaborately carved, but the finish seemed poor. Angelo removed it from the box, stood it on the floor and removed the floss. He inspected the container, checked everything for writing or other contents and then replaced the inner floss exactly as he had found it. Puzzled, he stared at the statue.

He was a spy, and a good one, which meant that he reported exactly what he saw and heard without trying to interpret the information. He gave the circumstances in which he had learned it, but that was all. And he knew that it was not for him to judge the relative merits of any imparted information. He could not make such a judgment. Angelo had no enemies and no cause. He did what he did for money and, if he thought about it at all, he merely wondered what possible use all the odd scraps and items he posted to the East Side box number could be.

But his instructions were clear; anything and everything dealing in the remotest fashion with the Orient. This parcel came under that heading and he would report it, but the report would be all the better for more details. And why should the girl in the Japanese legation send a statue to a shop, which, undoubtedly, would have a cupboard full of assorted Buddhas? And if they wanted more they could always obtain them through the usual channels.

Unless there was something very special about this particular statue.

Angelo was a realist, he was a spy because he needed the money, and his mind turned immediately to the possibility of smuggling. Carefully, he picked up the figure and examined it for possible hollowness, hidden plugs or other devices. It was opaque and it was hard to tell if it were hollow or not, but the weight suggested that it was solid. Inevitably he thought of opium.

He had never used the narcotic, but his hypnotic education had included details as to appearance and taste. The statue could have been made from the poppy derivative and either carved or pressed into shape. If that were the case the mystery was solved, for such an amount of opium would be worth a fortune on the underworld drug market.

Carefully, Angelo lifted the statue and

licked at the underside of the base. The surface felt slick and cold, something like the shell of an egg. He licked harder and this time was rewarded by a distinct taste. It was a blend of something between chocolate and raw meat and, whatever it was, it wasn't opium. He discovered that his tongue had left a slight depression on the surface. To cover it, he licked the base of the statue equally all over, then blew on the surface to dry it.

The examination had taken longer than he thought and he hurried as he repacked the parcel. The statue was made of some hard material coated with a softer film. The carving was too elaborate for the basic material to be soft, and the fuzzy finish proved the existence of a softer coating. So much he knew, but that was all he knew and all he could report.

Heating the blade of his knife he resealed the outer plastic, then swore as the keen blade slipped and nicked the ball of his thumb. The pain or the injury didn't worry him, but he didn't want to get blood on the wrapping. He examined it as he sucked the minor wound. No blood. The parcel, superficially, was exactly as he had received it.

Leaving the men's room he returned to the substrip and continued his journey to the Hudson terminal at the point where Broadway met Park Avenue. He checked the number of the Asian Antique shop from a vid book in a public booth and found it was about halfway down the avenue. He hesitated by a short-drop bus stop, noticed the queue and decided that it would be quicker to walk.

Halfway towards his destination someone stole the parcel.

It was quickly and neatly done.

Angelo felt someone bump into him, and, at the same time, the parcel shot forward from beneath his arm. The thief ran forward, caught it before it hit the ground and darted into the crowd of pedestrians.

After him ran Angelo.

He was no longer a young man, but he was still fit and he dived after the thief yelling for him to stop. The thief didn't stop. He didn't even look back, but wriggled between the pedestrians, the parcel gripped in both hands, his head bent and his shoulders hunched as he ran towards a maze of side streets leading from the river. A few people stared after him and one or two made an effort to follow. They soon gave up. Thieving was common and most criminals didn't hesitate to hit out when in danger of capture. Sometimes they were armed, and no one, in this day and age, wanted to get hurt or killed. They had too much to lose.

Angelo forced himself through the crowd intent on recovering the parcel. Personally, it didn't really affect him, but his pride as a messenger wouldn't let him give up without making an effort. He dived down an alley, caught a glimpse of the thief vanishing around a corner, threw himself in pursuit and swore as he found himself doubling back to the main street.

The exertion was telling on him, and his heart thudded against his ribs and the breath rasped in his throat as he merged with the crowd. He saw a flurry of movement at an intersection and a familiar figure darted across the avenue just as the lights changed colour. He was about to follow when a hand gripped his arm.

'Hold it!' The policeman jerked him backwards as a car swept past with a hum from its turbine. 'You wanta get yourself killed?'

'My parcel.' Angelo fought for breath as he tried to explain. 'I've got to recover that parcel.'

'Been robbed?' The policeman stared to where Angelo pointed. He could see nothing but the stream of traffic and the normal crowds. He shrugged and turned to the messenger. 'Nothing I can do, mister. Be more careful next time.'

'I . . . ' Angelo gasped and pressed his hand to his chest as pain tore at his heart. The cop stared at him, his face suddenly anxious.

'What's the matter, mister? You ill or something?'

Angelo couldn't answer.

4

The thief

Joe Leghorn wasn't surprised at the knock on the door; he'd been expecting it for three days now, but he took his time answering it just the same. He opened the door just as his landlord was about to beat again on the panel. Learhy blinked, looking foolish with his hand lifted as if to beat against empty air.

'You woke me up,' accused Joe. 'What do you want?'

'The rent.' Learhy was a man who came straight to the point. 'You owe me for three days now. Have you got it?'

'No.'

'I thought not.' Learhy stepped into the room. 'All right, Joe, collect your stuff and get out of here.'

'Now wait a minute,' pleaded Joe. 'Just give me a little more time and I'll pay you in full. Hell, man, you know how it is in my business. One day you haven't got it, the next you have. You know?'

'I know.' Learhy jerked his head towards the door. 'Out.'

'Just two days, Learhy.' Joe was getting desperate. 'Just two days. I've got something cooking that's going to pay off big. You'll get your money.'

'I'd better.' Learhy touched the tin badge that made a bright spot on his lapel. 'You try to gyp me, Joe, and I'll appeal to the Association. I don't pay protection for nothing.'

'I won't gyp you.' Joe had tangled with the Landlords' Protection Association before and they played rough. He forced himself to smile. 'You'll give me some time?'

'One day.' Learhy sucked at his bad teeth. 'You pay the rent by this time tomorrow or you go out on your ear. And don't try to sneak your stuff out. If you don't come across with the cash I'm keeping it.' He touched the badge again, scowled at his tenant, then went stumping down the stairs. Joe started to slam the door, thought better of it and closed it quietly instead. Tiredly, he sat on the rumpled bed and stared at the place he had called home for the past two years.

It wasn't much, just an eight by five cubicle, but it had its own door and its own ceiling light and gave a certain degree of privacy. The walls were of hardboard painted a dull, uninspired brown. A tall Perbox stood in one corner like an old-fashioned coffin and a rickety chair filled in at the foot of the bed. There were no windows; ventilation was provided by a grille over the door. The door itself could be opened by a kid with a hairpin, but that didn't matter. It took the pattern of his thumb to open the Perbox, and no one in their right mind would leave anything of value lying around. That's what the personal boxes were for.

The couple next door had fallen silent when Learhy had banged on the door; now they resumed their eternal arguments in penetrating whispers. He did night work; she didn't work at all. He wanted to get some sleep; she didn't see any fun in sitting around all day watching a man snore. He wanted to know why the hell she didn't get herself a job; she wanted to know just what kind of a woman he took her for. Such arguments usually ended in a screaming fight.

From the room to the other side came the fretful whining of a hungry child. Both whispers and whining were normal; when every word could be overheard people grew into the habit of whispering, and hunger was simply a part of growing up.

Irritably, Joe jabbed his thumb against the lock of the Perbox and took out his toilet articles. For a change the washroom was empty and he showered, shaved with depilatory cream, combed his thinning hair end rinsed out his spare shirt and underwear. The synthetic fabric was advertised to dry within five minutes and, with the help of the hot-air dryer, he managed to stay within four minutes of that time. The manufacturers must have used a blast furnace in order to justify their claim.

From his lodgings, habit carried him to the sleazy self-serve restaurant where he usually ate. A dollar bought him a half-pint of coffee in a paper cup and freedom to sit at one of the tables. Another bought him a shot of low-grade brandy from the alky dispenser. It wasn't good coffee, and the raw spirit that gave it flavour would have insulted any Frenchman, but it was the best he could afford.

Wedging his way between a fat man dressed in a conservative suit of maroon edged with yellow piping and a pale-faced com-sec chewing on a sandwich, Joe sipped his normal breakfast and stared at the two-hundred-inch tv screen hanging against one wall.

The item then showing was a flash from the assembly chamber of the World Council. Senator Sucamari was proposing a motion that the Calcutta project be given top priority. Senator Rayburn was opposing the motion. The scene seemed to annoy the fat man.

'Damn Chinese,' he snorted. 'They're nothing but a lot of bloodsucking leeches. First that big plant on Hainan; now they want to spend twice as much on another at Calcutta. It should be stopped.'

'Indians ain't Chinese,' said Joe.

'What's the difference?' demanded the fat man. 'They aren't white, are they?'

'Nothing wrong in providing food,' said Joe. 'Maybe you've never been hungry.'

'I've worked for every mouthful of food I've ever eaten,' snapped the fat man. 'I don't believe in charity, and neither does Rayburn. We can't be expected to keep pouring out money for the benefit of backward peoples. The Asiatics should look after themselves.'

'Sure,' said Joe. He didn't want an argument. 'You got a cigarette?'

'Never touch them,' said the fat man. 'I know they're supposed to be safe these days, but I never got the habit . . . Now, what this country needs is a strong man at the head who can tell these Chinese where to get off. It's time we began worrying about ourselves a little more and the world in general a little less.'

'Rayburn say that?' Joe lit a non-carcinogenic cigarette, one of his last. He ignored the expression on the fat man's face.

'He did. Say, what made you ask for a cigarette when you've got some?'

'Absent minded,' said Joe. 'I don't remember things so good before breakfast.'

'Breakfast?' The fat man looked startled. 'It's well past noon.'

'That's right.' Joe put down his empty cup. 'Breakfast time.'

Drawing on his cigarette, he returned his attention to the screen.

The newsfax boys had decided that the World Council had had enough free publicity and had switched over to a sponsored beauty contest. The girls, long legged, scantily dressed and superbly shaped, paraded across the screen in a blaze of colour, posturing and showing their teeth in exaggerated smiles. The smiles were important; the sponsor manufactured toothpaste.

Beauty was followed by humour. Prosper had managed to scrape up enough money to buy a minute of screen time in order to beg funds for his Alpha Project. His lined face with its bagged eyes surmounted by a ruff of white hair gave him the appearance of an intelligent dog. Both Prosper and his Portal were widely regarded as a joke and he was faded out during the second repeat of his address while the cameras gave a fifteen-second flash of the mess a Blue had made when he'd jumped from the top of a three-hundred-storey building to spatter on the concrete below.

There was no comment as to the reasons that had made a potential immortal take his own life.

Joe didn't even think about it. He was engrossed with his own worries. Learhy had meant exactly what he had said; either Joe scraped up some money today or tomorrow he would be dispossessed and probably beaten up as well. He sighed as he thought about it, almost wishing that he had a regular job. He had never taken to the idea of steady employment, preferring to use his dubious talents on various get-rich-quick schemes, which, somehow, had all failed to be as profitable as they should. Joe, in short, was a drifter, a petty criminal and a human parasite. He was forty years of age, looked fifty, and had known various degrees of poverty all his life.

He grunted and looked up as something hard jabbed against his ribs. The house cop, billy in hand, stared pointedly at Joe's empty cup.

'You finished, bud?'

'Just finished.'

'Then buy more or beat it.' The cop let his club thud softly against his thigh. 'You know the rules; no loitering.' He slapped the plastic tube against his leg again; he seemed to like the sound and feel. 'Nothing personal, you understand, but that's the way it's got to be. Some guys think they can sit in here all day for the price of a coffee.' The club reached towards the man in the maroon suit. The com-sec had already left, hurrying back to her machine and the endless programmes for the computers. 'That goes for you, too, fatso. Buy more or get moving and make room for others.'

'I'm going.' The fat man heaved himself to his feet and waddled from the restaurant. Joe, taking his time, sauntered to the change booth and cracked his last remaining bill into coins. He hesitated by the alky dispenser, then decided against another shot. He wanted the alcohol but couldn't afford it. He compromised by paying twice as much for a package of cigarettes, lit one and walked out into the street.

The area around the restaurant was a poor one, a collection of tumbledown brownstone houses converted by flimsy walls and sagging doors into a rabbit warren of man-made slums. The streets were full of children screaming and yelling as they played in the gutter. Older children, too grown-up for play, too young for work, lounged on steps and against walls, little knots of them huddled around dice and card games. Every window had a small window box containing a tired mass of vegetation, mostly perpetual spinach with sometimes a few carrots or broccoli to break the monotony. But no flowers. You can't eat flowers.

Joe hated the neighbourhood. He hated the smell of garbage, of cooking, of too many people living in too small an area. He had grown up in such an environment and his hope and dream was that, one day, he would be able to break away from it. It was a dream that had kept him single. Who wanted to be saddled with a wife and kids? The same dream had sent him running from his family as soon as he was old enough to make his own way. He wanted to make a fresh start and one day he would do it. Everything was in his favour; no dependent Blues to support, no wife, no kids, nothing. When his big chance came he was ready to grab it with both hands.

But he wished that it wasn't so long in coming.

A public videophone booth stood on the corner. Joe shut himself in, fed coins into the slot and punched a number. The screen flashed with colour and cleared to reveal a woman's face.

'Ajax Service Agency. Can — ' She broke off as she recognised him. 'Hello, Joe.'

'Hello, Margie. Got anything for me?'

'Some mail, all circulars.'

Margie owned a share-office and ran a twenty-four hour service taking messages, collecting mail, typing letters and providing an address to all the drifters who needed an office but couldn't afford one. Joe was listed as a trouble-shooter, a category that meant nothing but that he was willing to sell his services to anyone who needed them.

'Nothing else? Didn't Fred leave word for me?'

'Fred Wolfe?' Margie shook her head. 'I haven't heard from Fred in almost a week.'

'Hell!' Fred was a small-time operator who sold low-grade protection on a take-it-or-else basis to owners of Blue-staffed sweatshops. Sometimes he needed help and Joe had been relying on him. 'All right, Margie,' he said.

'So there's nothing doing. Thanks, anyway.' He was about to cut the connection when she remembered something.

'The rent, Joe,' she reminded. 'It's due tomorrow. Don't forget it.'

'I won't.' The screen turned blank on his scowl. Margie was like Learhy; she got her office rent or didn't provide an office. And without an office he couldn't stay in business.

Leaving the booth, he headed for the substrip terminal. Hanging around an area where poverty was the rule was a waste of time. No one had anything and there were a dozen applicants for every opportunity. To get money he had to go where money was, and it was worth the cost of the ride into town.

He left the substrip at the New Lincoln terminal and headed directly towards a coke dispenser. He wasn't really thirsty and he normally didn't touch the soft drink, but he'd fallen victim to a flashad and, for some reason he didn't know, he craved for a nice Coke. He wasn't alone. A half-dozen other travellers joined him, each eager to press money in the slot of the dispenser.

After the drink, Joe wandered up and down Park Avenue, staring enviously into the shops and at the expensively dressed customers. The Undersea Bureau had a double-display of sub-marine produce, dried kelp, molluscs, strange plants and other products of the underwater farms. Joe stared at a schematic of one of the domes, wondering what it was like to live in an inverted eggshell and go to work wearing diving dress.

'Interested?' A man in a sea-green and silver uniform smiled at him from the door. 'We've a few spots open for willing workers. Three-year contract, all found and a hundred dollars a day spending money. How about it?'

'No thanks.'

'Think again,' urged the man. 'A new farm down off the coast of Florida. Plenty of sunlight and plenty of shore leave.' He stepped forward and lowered his voice. 'Full recreation, too, get me?' His wink and nudge were expressive.

'What's the working depth?' said Joe then, as the man hesitated. 'Not that it matters. I've got a bad pump and couldn't pass the medical.'

'You don't look a heart case,' said the man. 'Tell you what I'll do. You sign up and, if the medical flunks you, you keep the retainer. Is it a deal?'

'I'll think about it.' Joe had no intention of accepting the offer. There was nothing wrong with his heart, but even if there was, the medic would still have passed him. Life in the domes was tough, though, from what he had heard, a smart man with the right connections could clean up if he had a way with cards and dice. Gambling was the main recreation of the undersea workers, and most of them finished their contract time as broke as when they'd first signed on.

Thinking about money reminded him of why he was here. Picking a discarded newspaper from a trash basket, he walked down to the National Bank and concentrated on business.

People are creatures of habit. When a man draws money from a bank he will invariably count it, even though the teller has already done it twice before his eyes. Usually a man will hesitate to recount it right away; most of them do it while on their way from the counter, holding the cash in their hands and satisfying themselves as to the amount. Some are slower than others, some more careless or perhaps simply in a hurry.

Joe was waiting for someone who would still be holding his money when he emerged into the street. When that happened he intended to make a quick snatch-and-run, trusting to luck and the crowds to make good his getaway. The newspaper was merely for camouflage and to hide his features.

It was a good plan and might even have worked had circumstances been just right, but Joe, looking in his rumpled suit of green and orange checks like a shop-soiled parrot, attracted too much attention. A bank guard saw him leaning against the wall reading his newspaper. A half an hour later he was still there. The guard, employed to be suspicious, walked over and jerked his thumb.

'On your way, mister.'

'What's with you?' Joe was annoyed. He folded the newspaper so as to hide the peephole he had made, stuck it in his pocket and glared at the guard.

'The bank own the street now?'

'No. It just doesn't like people hanging about outside. Just move someplace else, that's all.'

'I'm waiting for a friend,' said Joe stubbornly, but he recognised defeat. No matter how the argument turned out he was beaten. If he insisted on staying the guard would watch him like a hawk; if he moved too far away his chance of a snatch-and-run would be lost. Cursing the guard and his luck in general, he crossed the avenue to the other side.

And saw Angelo with his parcel.

What followed then was automatic. Joe didn't recognize Angelo's uniform as belonging to the World Council, but he did recognise it as a uniform. To Joe a uniformed messenger in this area meant money, a shop employee with a parcel of goods sent on approval, a servant of the idle rich, a chauffeur perhaps picking up some expensive item. It had to be expensive. Park Avenue didn't specialise in low-cost items. Whatever it was, it would be valuable.

And Joe was desperate for money.

His shoulder bumped into the messenger at the same moment as the heel of his hand slammed against the parcel, knocking it forward. Two quick steps and he was off, the parcel in his hands and his face unseen by the man he'd robbed. The rest was routine; quick wriggle through the crowd and into a side street, down which he raced like a scalded cat. Then doubling back into the avenue where the crowd would shield him from view.

Luck was with him and he managed to cross the avenue just before the road became clogged with traffic. Safe on the far side he dropped to a fast walk, looking like a man with an errand and with little time to spare. After a quarter of a mile he relaxed, smiling with success. He lost the smile as a hand fell his shoulder.

5

The statue changes hands

It was a big hand, ornamented with rings, and it belonged to a plump, smiling man dressed in flaming reds and yellows so that he resembled an old-time clown. He chuckled at Joe's expression.

'Now, now, my friend,' he said. 'No need to be alarmed. Not when the Spot Quiz is offering you the opportunity to win the magnificent prize of one million dollars.' He rolled the words as if he liked the taste. 'One million dollars, friend, and all yours if you can answer five simple questions. Now, just step this way and try for a fortune.'

Joe relaxed. The Spot Quiz procedure was simple and well-known; a recording van selected a site, a passer-by was approached and the fun began.

'Hurry, friend.' The Quiz Master was impatient. 'Let's not waste time. Just step before the cameras and let's see if you're going to be the winner of that big, beautiful, million-dollar prize.'

Joe stepped forward. To any criminal a crowd offers the best hiding place, and no one around could know that the parcel he carried wasn't his own. And there was always the chance that he might win. If he did, he would be the first one. The Spot Quiz was tough; no one had ever walked off with the prize, and the betting was that no one ever would. But there was no harm in trying. He smiled as he faced the cameras.

'Your name, friend?' The genial Quiz Master pointed a directional mike towards Joe's lips. It was out of range of the cameras and his own throat mike was hidden beneath a flowing cravat. The Spot Quiz took pains to appear natural.

'Joe Leghorn.' The reply was automatic.

'And your employment?'

'Trouble-shooter. I'm in the book.' There was, Joe thought, no harm in trying for a little free advertising.

'So you're a trouble-shooter. That means that if anyone is in trouble they can hire you to get them out of it. Right?'

'That's right,' said Joe. 'I'm licensed, too.'

'Of course. And how long have you been helping your fellow men?'

'Twenty years,' said Joe quickly. 'And I've never failed a client yet. I . . . '

'Good. Good.' The Quiz Master had a voice like thick cream. 'Very interesting, I'm sure. Well, you know the rules, Joe. Just answer five consecutive questions correctly, and within five seconds of asking, and you will walk away from here with a certified cheque for one million dollars.' He held the outsized cheque so that Joe could see it. 'Nice, isn't it?'

'I'll say so.' Joe's mouth watered at the thought of what he could do with a million dollars.

'Now for the first question, Joe, an easy one I'm sure. The first question is this. Which organisation had its headquarters on the site now occupied by the World Council?' The plump man smiled. 'You know the answer to that one, don't you?' He stressed the first two words.

'UNO,' gasped Joe.

'Correct! The United Nations Organisation was taken over and incorporated into the World Council. Now for question number two. The second question, Joe, is this. The penalty for murder is the same as for crippling mayhem. What is it?'

'Forced labour for the full term of natural life,' said Joe. He knew the answer to that one. 'And longevity treatment refused,' he added quickly.

'Again correct! Now, Joe, listen carefully to the next question. The third question is this. If it is 12.00 hours here in New York, what is the time in London England?'

'Uh?' Joe blinked, his mind racing. He knew that the time was different, just as it was between New York and San Francisco, and he guessed it was about the same. But was it forward or back? He took a chance. 'Seventeen hundred hours.'

'And for the third time correct!' The Quiz Master seemed bursting with joy at the prospect of having to hand over the million-dollar prize. 'Three questions answered and two to go. Two more correct answers, Joe, and you can take home that great, big, wonderful cheque for a million dollars. Are you married, Joe?'

'No.'

'With a million dollars to spend I bet that you won't stay single for long.' The plump man gave a deep belly laugh. 'Speaking of marriage, Joe, what is the waiting period for divorce in this state?'

'Three . . . ' Joe paused. The question was the waiting period for *divorce*, not marriage. He had almost fallen into the trap. 'Six weeks,' he said. 'From time of application to dissolution.'

'Wonderful! Again correct!' The Quiz Master reacted as if Joe had just told him the answer to the riddle of the Sphinx. 'Four questions answered, Joe, and only one to go for that one million dollars. For the last question, Joe, the one which may make you a millionaire.' Deliberately he paused so as to build up the tension. 'Give the exact definition of a parsec.' He began counting off the seconds. 'One . . . Two . . . Three . . . '

'A part of a second,' said Joe

desperately. He didn't know the answer, but anything was better than remaining silent. The Quiz Master with his damn counting didn't give a man a chance to think, and the crowds pressing around weren't any help, either.

' . . . Five!' The plump man looked regretful. 'Sorry, Joe, but you've failed to answer the fifth and last question. A parsec is an astronomical unit of length corresponding to a parallax of one second of arc and is about three and one third light years. That was the answer I wanted, Joe, and that was the answer you didn't give.'

'How the hell was I supposed to know that?' Joe felt furious. He'd practically felt that cheque in his hands.

'Any astronomer would have known it,' pointed out the Quiz Master. 'And I'll bet that there are a dozen people in this audience who know it, too.' He beamed at the crowd. 'But, as a consolation prize, the sponsors of the Spot Quiz are giving you this voucher which may be exchanged at any store for a thousand dollars worth of Miracle Maid Products.' He handed

Joe the voucher and turned to someone else in the crowd. 'And now, you, madam, or is it miss? Your name is?'

Joe, forgotten, eased his way out of the crowd. He wasn't too disappointed; the voucher could be sold at most stores for half its face value, so the quiz hadn't been a total loss. And he still had the parcel.

★ ★ ★

Safe at home he examined it, cursing at what he found. It wasn't jewels, perfume, gold or silver ware, all of which he could have disposed of with a minimum of effort at a good profit. Instead, it was just a lousy statue in a trick box. Disgustedly, Joe sat down on the bed and stared at it.

Elementary caution had dictated the wearing of gloves when he opened the parcel; he didn't want to cover the contents with his fingerprints, nor did he want to dust his hands with any skin-ink powder it might have contained. Valuable parcels were often trapped with the powder, which turned purple on contact with the skin. A suspect would have a hard job explaining away stained hands. Now he sat and examined his find, turning the Buddha over in his gloved hands as he tried to estimate its worth.

He was still examining it when Learhy walked into the room.

The landlord was a little drunk and inclined to be argumentative. He glared at the wrapping, the box and the statue, and immediately became suspicious.

'So I was right,' he said. 'I guessed that you'd try and pull a fast one. Now I catch you packing up ready to sneak out while owing me the rent. Well, we'll see about that.' He made a grab for the box, then swore as Joe knocked aside his arm.

'Lay off,' said Joe. With money in his pocket he could afford to be independent. 'I'm not clearing out, though it would serve you right if I did. No one but a fool would pay the rent you ask for this rat trap.' He returned the statue to the box, snapped shut the lid and rewrapped it. 'Got any money?'

'Money?' Learhy looked blank.

'That's what I said. Real money, the kind you carry in your pocket.' Joe held out the voucher. 'This is worth at least five hundred. Take what I owe you and give me the change.'

'You kidding?' Learhy took the voucher, held it up to the light and pursed his lips in a soundless whistle as he checked the watermark. 'This is genuine.'

'Sure it's genuine.' Joe glared his impatience. 'Are you going to cash it for me, or do I take it someplace else?'

'How did you get it, Joe?' Learhy was suspicious.

'I won it.' Joe reached for the voucher. 'If you don't want it I'll find someone who does.'

'I'll cash it,' said Learhy hastily. He knew that he could squeeze six hundred for it from a storekeeper he knew.

Slowly he counted out a sheaf of greasy notes. 'What you got in the parcel, Joe?'

'Heirlooms.' Joe picked up the money, counted it and tucked it into his empty wallet. 'You interested in heirlooms, Learhy?'

'Not me,' said the landlord. 'Johanasen might be.'

'That robber!'

'You could try somewhere else, but Johanasen's interested in most things.' Learhy winked. 'And it's cash down and no questions.'

'This stuff is legitimate.'

'Sure.' Learhy was quick to agree. 'So it's legitimate. But try Johanasen, all the same.'

* * *

A long time ago one of Johanasen's forebears had been born on the shores of the Baltic, but he had passed down little but his name. The present holder looked more Armenian than Norwegian, a big, fat, greasy-looking man with hooded eyes and a perpetually-stubbled chin. He was listed as a general dealer and ran a communal lodging house and soup kitchen in a rambling warehouse he owned. One corner of it was occupied by his business premises. He also ran a sweatshop and kept a dozen Blues busy twelve hours a day sorting junk and shredding rags, for which labour he paid them in bed and board. Sometimes one of his workers would quit the sweatshop, preferring to starve in the gutter or queue long hours for the government handout rather than work his fingers raw. Johanasen didn't mind; there were always plenty more Blues to make up the number.

He came to the counter of his shop as Joe pushed through the door and folded his meaty arms on the wood as he stared at the parcel.

'Hello, Joe,' he greeted. 'How's business?'

'I'm living.' Joe put down the parcel and stared at the dealer. 'What's the matter with your face?'

'The cuts?' Johanasen lifted one big hand and gently touched his cheek. 'Had an argument with one of my dependents. She swung at me with a rake before taking off.' He spat thoughtfully on the dirty floor. 'Some people don't know the meaning of gratitude, Joe. They bite the hand that feeds them. But she'll be sorry. That I promise.'

'Sure,' said Joe. He knew all about the sweatshop and flophouse. He could even guess the reason for the argument.

'Yes,' said Johanasen softly. 'She'll be sorry. I'll teach the bitch to show her claws. Goddamn Blues, you can't trust a one.' He changed the subject. 'Got a nice suit just come in, Joe. Real sharp. Fit you like a glove, cheap, too.'

'Not interested, thanks all the same.'

'No? Then what are you interested in?' Johanasen looked at the parcel. 'Come on, Joe, open up.'

Joe unwrapped the parcel. He was still wearing his gloves and he kept them on as he opened the box. Johanasen stared expressionlessly at the Buddha.

'It's a real, genuine work of art,' said Joe. 'Worth a fortune to a museum or a collector.' He had spent some time before coming to the dealer window-shopping at antique shops. He had seen a set of carved ivory chessmen and the price had shocked him. If the box and the statue were worth only half that, then he was in gravy.

'Junk,' said Johanasen.

'Like hell it's junk!' Joe was indignant. 'You don't pick up junk on Park Avenue.'

He bit his lips, realizing that he had said too much. 'This is the real stuff. Look at that box, all carved and inlaid. You don't see work like that outside a museum, and you know it.'

'Still junk,' said the dealer. He made no move to touch the articles. 'Why are you wearing gloves, Joe?'

'Hands are cold.'

'Feet, too?'

'I don't get it.' Joe frowned at the dealer. 'It's cold outside.'

Johanasen shrugged and, reaching under the counter, produced a pair of gloves and a jeweller's glass. He switched on an overhead light, donned the gloves and screwed the glass into his eye. Carefully, he examined both the box and the statue.

'These things are clean,' he said after a while. 'No skin-ink, anyway. Did you expect the parcel to be trapped?'

'Of course not.' Joe registered indignation. 'Why should I?'

'I'm asking the questions, Joe.'

'You're asking too many damn questions!' Joe was annoyed. He didn't like

Johanasen, and he didn't like being played with cat and mouse. The dealer had a bad reputation; he was fond of buying stolen property from teenagers then blackmailing them into obedience. One day he would end up with a knife in his ribs. 'I'm offering something for sale,' said Joe. 'You want it or not?'

'Two hundred dollars.'

'I'm getting deaf,' said Joe. 'I didn't hear that.'

'You heard me.' Johanasen flipped the box with the tip of one gloved finger. 'Stuff like this has no value, not unless I know more about it.'

'It's robbery!' Joe was disgusted. 'Hell, I could walk into hock shop and pledge it for five times what you offered.'

'Then why don't you?' Johanasen straightened and replaced the jeweller's glass and gloves under counter. 'Go ahead, Joe, what's keeping you?'

He knew as well as Joe did what was keeping him. Hock shops were legitimate; the continual police inspections took care of that. Even if the contents of the parcel hadn't been wired around, and it was almost certain that they had, Joe would still have to thumbprint the receipt. As a registered trouble-shooter his prints were on file at police headquarters, and to attach his mark to a receipt for money received for stolen goods was only delaying the inevitable.

But he wasn't defeated yet. 'So I can't take it to a hock shop. All right. But that doesn't mean I'm going to let you rob me. I'd rather dump the stuff in the river.'

'That's silly.' Johanasen shook his head. 'That's really silly.'

'Not to me it isn't.' Joe reached out for the parcel. The dealer gripped his arm.

'Take it, easy, Joe. You can maybe up the price with some information. Park Avenue, you said? Now why don't you tell me all about it?'

Joe sighed and told him.

Johanasen listened without change of expression. He knew as well as Joe that only the best was to be found on the Avenue, and he knew, much better than Joe, the probable value of what he had. Ivory, real ivory, was scarce. The statue was open to doubt, but the colour was about right for old ivory, and there was no doubt as to the box itself.

Lang Ki, down in Chinatown, would be willing to act as agent and sell the item to some rich collector who wouldn't be too curious.

'Tell you what I'll do,' said Johanasen. 'I'll give you five hundred and take a chance.'

'You don't take chances,' said Joe. 'This thing is worth a lot more than that and you know it.'

'It could be hot,' reminded the dealer. 'I could lose out on the deal.'

'Not while you can dicker with the insurance companies.' Joe reached towards the box. 'Maybe I can make a deal with them myself.'

'Relax, Joe.' Johanasen produced a roll of bills, knowing how the actual sight of money will weaken a man's resolve. 'Take the five hundred now and let me handle it. If I can pass it off without trouble and at a profit I'll cut you in for the same again. Is it a deal?'

It was the best he could get and Joe knew it. Sullenly he took the money, then hesitated, the notes in his hand.

'When will I know? About the extra, I mean.'

'A few days; these things take time.'

'I'll drop in tomorrow, just to remind you.' Joe pocketed the money and stepped into the street. A woman passed him, head lowered and a bundle in her arms. The bundle was alive. Joe paused to light a cigarette and stared after her, wondering what it must be like to be a woman with a kid, broke and homeless, with no one to help and with winter just around the corner. Hell, he guessed, what with the worry and all. Shrugging, he walked down the street. It wasn't his business.

The Blue wasn't any of his business, either. The man had followed him from Johanasen's, hanging back like a dog, waiting, Joe knew, for the butt of his cigarette. A lot of people had fun that way with the Blues, leading them on and then, at the last minute, throwing the butt into a puddle or trampling it to unusable ruin. Joe didn't act that way. Taking the cigarette from between his lips, he held it out to the Blue. The man looked at it, then at Joe, his eyes reflecting his hunger.

'Go ahead,' said Joe. 'I won't bite.'

'Thanks, mister.' The Blue scuttled forward, lithe as a young man, and took the cigarette. He backed away as if expecting a kick.

Looking at him, Joe felt a touch of unaccustomed compassion. There, he thought, but for he grace of God, go I. He corrected himself. There, by the grace of God, I shall go. Father Rosen had taught him that when he had once dropped in at the mission for a handout. It was a sobering thought. He gave the man a dollar and headed for the nearest bar.

6

The horror begins

Sam Falkirk sat at his desk and tried to convince himself that he was doing work of vital necessity and great responsibility. He didn't succeed. The necessity was there, he supposed; someone had to be in charge of the policing of the World Council buildings, and the responsibility was there, too. As Major Hendricks, his immediate superior, had once told him, 'you wipe their noses, hold their hands and do everything but tuck them into bed at night.' He had been talking about the senators and their staffs.

Responsible or not, Sam had noticed that none of his superiors felt it necessary for them to be stationed at the World Council Headquarters. They were at the Polar Base or supervising the examination teams scattered over the globe. Sam would have liked to be one of them.

Keeping an eye on the nations so as to make sure that no one tried to secretly re-arm was a useful job. One day he might be allowed to join them. One day. Even the Health Army had more to do than he had, despite his title. At least they had to be on constant alert, and there was always the chance of their being sent on an extermination party to wage war against the insect life, threatening the food production. But Sam admitted, they probably were as bored at times as he was now.

At the moment Sam was drawing up the duty roster for the coming week. Mike, his secretary, a rookie cop who hadn't yet worn his uniform into creases, reached out to the intercom as it hummed its attention signal.

'Captain Falkirk's office.' He listened to the voice from the machine, the directional speaker throwing a cone of clarity about his head and a muffled squawking everywhere else, an arrangement that permitted official business to be conducted privately in the presence of outsiders. He snapped off the machine and turned to Sam. 'Report from courier control, sir. One of their messengers, Angelo Augustine, collapsed on Park Avenue a short while ago. He's been taken to the General Mercy Hospital.'

'Angelo!' Sam stared his surprise. 'What was the trouble?'

'Control didn't say, sir.'

'And you didn't ask.' Sam shook his head with exaggerated severity. 'How can we make out a report without all the facts, Mike? The messenger is one of our people and comes under our jurisdiction.' He drummed his fingers on his desk. 'Get to work on it, Mike. All information as fast as possible.'

'Yes, sir.' Mike reached for the video-phone and dialed. The screen lit up with the image of the switchboard operator. 'Police, here,' said Mike. 'Get me the General Mercy Hospital. Casualty department.' He waited as the screen blurred then steadied to reveal a new image.

'General Mercy Hospital. Can I help you?' The nurse was young and very pretty. Mike smiled at her as he introduced himself.

'You have a patient, one of our messengers, a man named Angelo Augustine. Would you tell me his condition, please?'

'One moment, sir.' The screen hummed and showed a blank wall. The nurse returned. 'Condition of patient is critical. Preliminary diagnosis is cardiac thrombosis with bronchial complications.'

'Thank you.' Mike cut the connection. 'Heart,' he said in answer to Sam's questioning stare. 'His pump must have given out on him.' He dialled the operator again and asked for police headquarters. He introduced himself, asked his questions, fumed at the delay and hit the cut-off switch as if he hated it.

'They don't like us,' he said. He was referring to the local police. 'The time they take to answer a few simple questions!'

'They're probably busy,' said Sam. 'What did they say?'

'Not much. Apparently Angelo simply collapsed just as he was about to cross Park Avenue. An officer standing close to him called an ambulance. They promised to send in a report as soon as they could.' He shrugged. 'It's heart trouble right enough.'

'Is it?' Sam was thoughtful. 'I spoke to him only a little while ago, and he seemed all right then.' He reached for his phone, asked for and was connected with the medical centre, spoke to records and then asked for the resident physician. The face which appeared on the screen was old, wise and with an innate good humour. Doctor Jelks could afford to be good humoured. The senators and staff of the World Council demanded the best medical attention they could get, and the resident physician was one of the best.

'Hello, Sam. How's your health?'

'Blooming.' Sam and Jelks were old friends. He became serious. 'Something rather unpleasant has come up. A messenger, Angelo Augustine, collapsed on Park Avenue and was taken to the General Mercy Hospital. Their diagnosis is heart trouble. Records tell me that you checked him only two weeks ago.' He paused, letting his question hang on the air.

'You think I boo-booed, is that it?' Jelks shook his head. 'The trust some people have in the old medic. Hell, Sam, if I passed him as fit, then he was fit. You know that.'

'He's in a bad way,' reminded Sam. 'His condition is critical. Cardiac thrombosis and complications.' He paused again. 'Maybe you'd better check.'

'I'll do that, and then I'll come up for a personal apology.' Jelks' anger was artificial. 'Expect me immediately.'

★   ★   ★

He took a little longer than immediately, and by the time the doctor arrived Sam had discovered the switch in assignments. He was about to phone the Japanese legation when Jelks came hurrying into the office. On the videophone he had seemed perfectly normal; it was only in the direct lighting that his pallor revealed itself for what it was. He sat down, his left hand holding a thick file blotched with the blue star. He was worried.

'Were you joking, Sam?' He answered

his own question. 'No, of course you weren't, but the thing is incredible.' He opened the file. 'I checked Augustine myself only a few days ago and the man was as fit as could be expected for a man of his age. He had the full treatment, too, electrocardiograph, electroencephalograms, blood tests, the works. He was good for at least another ten years, and his heart was sound.'

'And yet he's in hospital with a critical heart condition,' pointed out Sam. 'Something isn't making sense, doc.' He pushed forward the phone. 'Maybe you'd better check yourself.'

'I will.' Jelks grabbed the instrument and dialled the number. He snapped at the receptionist, demanded to be put in contact with the doctor in charge, settled for someone else and made no attempt to hide his impatience. From then on the conversation grew technical and bristled with medical jargon. As it progressed Jelks grew more subdued and, when he finally cut the connection, he had lost much of his good humour.

'I can't believe it.' Jelks stared blankly

at the file he had brought with him. 'His heart couldn't have been in that condition.'

'Tell me.' Sam had tried to follow the conversation and had become lost. 'How bad is he?'

'Damn bad. They've bypassed his heart with an exciter and are filtering his blood.' Jelks beat his hand softly against the wad of papers on his lap. He suddenly looked every day of his hundred and eleven years of age. 'I've got to go over to the hospital, Sam, you can see that, can't you? If I slipped up over Augustine, then I may have slipped over others. I can't take risk or expect them to take it. I've got to be sure.'

'I understand. Mike will arrange transport.' Sam hesitated. He was thinking of Carmen. 'You said he was bad, Jelks; just how bad did you mean? Is he going to die?'

'He shouldn't.' Jelks was impatient to get away. 'Not if I know my business and the hospital know theirs. But then he shouldn't have collapsed, either.' He looked at Sam. 'Thinking of his family?'

'Yes.'

'They can't do anything. They can't even see him, not yet. But I suppose they'll have to be told.'

'I'll tell them,' said Sam. It was a duty he didn't relish.

★ ★ ★

The Augustines lived in a small, downtown house, one of a row of identical buildings squeezed together as if for mutual support. It was late when Sam arrived and found that, as usual, the bad news had travelled before him. Mario, Augustine's grandfather, opened the door and ushered him into a cluttered living room. Two other Blues were sitting on chairs, Evelyn, Angelo's mother, and Tonio, his father. All three of the Blues looked about the same age.

'We heard about it,' said Mario. 'The hospital phoned us. It's a bad thing to happen, Sam.'

'I know. Is Carmen home yet?'

'She's upstairs with Clarissa.' Mario looked worried. 'She's taken it hard, Sam.'

'Clarissa?' Sam dropped his uniform cap on a chair and lit a cigarette. 'She'll get over it. After all, it isn't as if Angelo were dead. He'll be as good as new in a little while.' He wished that he could feel as confident as he sounded.

'I hope so.' Mario crossed the room to where a large television set emitted a soft blur of sound and colour and switched it off. The sudden cessation of noise was startling. Evelyn rose from where she had been sitting by the window.

'You'll want to see Carmen,' he said. 'I'll get her.' She looked at the other two Blues. 'Mario, you'd better stay with Clarissa. Tonio, you can help me in the kitchen.' She changed her mind. 'Better still, you entertain Sam while I make some coffee. You'd like some coffee, wouldn't you Sam?' As a question it was simply window dressing; she had gone before he could answer. Her daughter entered the room shortly afterwards.

Carmen was a product of the merging of two races and had retained the best qualities of both. Her hair and eyes were of a deep unusual black, her skin white and flawless, her figure belonged on the tv and tri-di theatre screens and her poise and assurance were to be envied.

Now she had lost her poise and her eyes were red from weeping.

'I phoned the hospital again,' she said dully. 'No change.'

'Jelks will phone as soon as there is anything definite to report,' said Sam. He turned as Evelyn entered the room, a tray bearing cups, sugar, cream and coffee in her hands. There was also a pile of small cakes. 'How's Clarissa now?'

'Sleeping.' Evelyn set down the tray. 'She'll be all right when she wakes. It was shock more than anything else. We haven't had a serious illness in the family since my brother died.' She busied herself with the cups. 'I hope you like these cakes. I made them from a new recipe, yeast flour mixed with dried algae. They're supposed to be full of nourishment.'

'I'll eat them.' Sam knew that she was talking more to fill in the silence than for any real need to communicate. He bit into one of the cakes. 'Good.'

'Are they? I'm so glad.' Evelyn looked at the other Blue. 'Come on, Tonio, I need you in the kitchen.' Obediently, he followed her from the room.

It was crude and, at any other time, Sam would have felt slightly a mused at the obvious manoeuvring.

The tricks of the elders to leave young couples on their own hadn't altered much over the centuries, but this time it was more than that. More than years separated the Blues from normal people. There was a change of outlook, a tranquility and calmness unknown to the young.

Angelo was very ill, maybe dying, and they probably felt very sorry about it, but it wasn't the same sorrow that tormented Carmen and her mother. They could neither be wholly in sympathy with it or truly understand it. Only Sam could do that, and he had been left alone to comfort her.

For, to a person in grief, love is the greatest comfort there is.

Carmen felt it, too, and she was awkward as she poured the coffee. Sam,

102

trying to fill a vacuum, switched on the television. Together, they sat and looked at the screen.

'The Spot Quiz.' said Carmen listlessly. 'I wonder if they ever have to pay out the prize money?'

'I doubt it.' Sam was cynical. 'The Quiz Master is smart and probably holds a degree in psychology. The way he operates is obvious. First, he selects a contender, finds out just what he does asks him a few simple questions a moron could answer, then knocks him out by asking him something totally outside his field.'

'Like that man?' Carmen adjusted a control on the handset and the sound grew in volume.

'Yes. He's a trouble-shooter. The last question will probably be on something like geology or nuclear physics. Something quite a few people can answer, but not him. That makes the question seem fair.' Sam nodded at the success of his prophecy. 'You see? How would a man like that know what a parsec is?'

'Clever,' said Carmen without interest.

She sat before the screen, staring at it without looking at it. 'Sam,' she said abruptly. 'Is father going to die?'

'Of course not.'

'Don't lie to me!' She turned towards him, suddenly fierce. 'Why do people insist on lying? If he's going to die, then why not say so? Does it make it any the less true by denying it?'

'Steady.' Sam took her hands between his own. 'He isn't dead yet,' he reminded. 'And there's no reason to think that he will die at all.'

'There was no reason to think that he'd collapse, either.' Carmen was bitter. She squeezed his hands in sudden contrition. 'Sorry, Sam. I guess my nerves are all on edge.'

'Isn't that natural?'

'Don't misunderstand me, Sam.' She looked directly into his eyes. 'I'm no Pollyanna. I think a lot of my father, but it goes deeper than that. There's my mother and Tonio and his wife, and Mario, too. What's going to become of them if father dies?'

'They'll get by,' he said awkwardly. 'But

why look on the black side? Angelo isn't dead; why talk as if he was?'

'Now or ten years, what's the difference?' Carmen was deliberately hurting herself, and Sam knew it. 'Legal death or actual death, the problem's the same. Mother's getting old and is about due for treatment. That'll make four of them, Sam. Four dependent Blues. What sort of a future have they to look forward to?'

And, thought Sam grimly, what sort of a future have you? Marriage was one way out, but who wanted to take on such a burden? And Carmen wasn't the type of girl to run out and leave her people to starve.

'You must think I'm a heel,' she said. 'Do you?'

'You are a woman. All women are realists.'

'And all men know how to dodge the point at issue.' She withdrew her hands. 'What do you think of me, Sam?'

'I think that you are beautiful,' he said, then stopped. He was no prude and no stranger to the opposite sex. He had even been in love a couple of times when younger, fortunately with women who, at the time, had had more sense than himself. More sense or a greater love of security. They had wanted children and he hadn't. He still didn't. But in a world where children were now an economic necessity, marriage without them was unthinkable.

'Flatterer!' Carmen smiled, pleased at his compliment, used to them as she must have been. She became serious. 'Sam, should the worst happen you — know what I mean — what shall I do?'

'If Angelo should die?' Sam switched off the tv and faced the girl. 'Well, he's insured, of course?'

'The usual policy,' she admitted. 'Lump sum at death if death should occur before treatment. Smaller sum and cost of treatment guaranteed. But it's all we have, Sam.'

'You have the house,' he reminded. There would be no pension, of course, pensions were a thing of the past. 'You could use the insurance money to convert the building and then let off the rooms.' He frowned at the cluttered living room. 'I'm surprised that you haven't done it before. This place is large enough to bring in a fairly good income. And then, naturally, you could always get married.'

'Yes,' she said softly. 'I could, couldn't I?' There was no mistaking the invitation in her eyes. Sam wavered, feeling a peculiar sense of the grotesque.

Reaction, he guessed, the after-math of an emotional storm and the urgings of nature, always trying in one way or another to restore the population. One man dead or dying, one man lost, balance the equation with a new marriage and plenty more offspring.

The curse was that he was in love with the girl and he knew it.

'Angelo will be all right,' he said quickly. 'You'll see. You'll both be laughing over this in a little while.' He was talking banalities and knew it, but it helped to fill the silence and ease the strain. He was glad when Evelyn knocked on the door and called to him.

'Sam. You're wanted on the phone.'

It was Jelks and his face, on the screen, was grim. 'Glad to catch you, Sam,' he said. 'I was afraid that you'd left. How's the family?'

'As you would expect. What's new?' He guessed the answer. 'Angelo's dead?'

'Yes, Sam. Angelo's dead.'

Jelks lifted his arm, the movement betraying the surgical cover-skin he wore. 'I've just finished the autopsy.'

'Was it heart failure?' Sam almost hoped it wasn't. To pass an unfit man as fit was a mistake that would cost Jelks more than his job. Human life now, as never before, was sacred.

'Depends on what you mean by heart failure,' said Jelks. 'A man shot through the pump could be said to have died of heart failure; if his heart hadn't stopped he'd still be living.'

'Well, then?'

'Angelo didn't die a normal death, Sam. Something killed him.'

'Murder?' Sam was incredulous. 'Is that what you're saying?'

'I don't know.' Jelks looked baffled. 'Murder implies a human adversary and so I just don't know. But I'm positive about one thing. Angelo Augustine didn't die a normal death.'

The horror had begun.

7

Search for Janice

The horror was the thing Sucamari had brought back with him from the Orient, smuggled in his diplomatic bag. A simple thing on the face of it, an inlaid box of ivory and mother of pearl containing a statue of Buddha nested on protective floss. Even had it been inspected at the customs it was innocent enough, the sort of thing that any traveller from the East might purchase as a curiosity or, as in the case of Sucamari, as an item to add to his collection. For the horror wasn't the box, nor the floss, nor the statue itself. It was in the substance that coated it.

Well over a century ago men had first toyed with the concept of using the smallest allies. Of turning from the big to the almost invisible, the tiny bacteria instead of the tearing destruction of explosives. In itself the concept wasn't new. Long before diseased women had been sent among enemy troops to weaken them with infection, but then, as earlier, the weapon had been two-edged. Infection, once released, spread. Bacteria has no friends. Disease, once released, would be impartial to all, and both sides would suffer. A victory under those circumstances would be a Pyrrhic one, and now, as lever before, any nation stooping to bacteriological warfare would suffer ghastly retaliation. The World Police would see to that from their Polar Base where the alphabet bombs were stored. Such a nation would simply cease to exist.

But what if the disease could be made selective? And, better still, what if the disease didn't appear to be that at all?

Sucamari thought that he had found the answer.

He sat in his legation and dreamed the old dreams of conquest. Not the old-fashioned conquest of treasure and slaves, but a new, infinitely more valuable conquest of land. Empty land living space for the teeming millions that surged and pressed in the Orient, increasing their already fabulous numbers with a passing of each hour. War was bad, he admitted that. War was wasteful, and now the world could not afford waste of any description. But a quiet elimination of peoples was something else.

Sucamari leaned back in his chair, his face for once devoid of shielding smile. He was no national hero, no official agent, but he was far more dangerous than either. In a way, he was one of the most dangerous types of men on Earth. He was an idealistic fanatic, a man who was so firmly convinced that he was right that he would stop at literally nothing to gain his own ends. And though he worked for the benefit of the Orient he knew that his own government would be the first to punish him should a hint of what he intended leak out.

Fortunately for the world such men were few, and those in high positions fewer still. In all the Orient only he and a handful of the true Samurai, the old warrior class of Japan, dreamed the dream of bloodless victory that would give the world to the East.

A bell chimed from the wall-clock and he started, checking the time against his watch. It was later than he had thought. Rising, he entered the outer office. Nagati, his eternal book on his lap, waited in the anteroom. He straightened as Sucamari crossed to the desk and opened a drawer.

'It is gone.' He spoke in Japanese.

'Good.' Despite his aide's assurance, Sucamari checked for himself. 'Later today you will contact the Asian Antique shop and inform them that there has been a mistake. Early tomorrow you will recover the parcel and do what you have to do. Be sure and return in time for your normal duties.' He glanced at his watch again. 'What time did Janice leave?'

'Early; she was gone before we arrived from the chamber.' Nagati frowned as if something troubled him. 'There is something wrong with that girl. She works as if in a dream and I have had to speak to her about it.' His fingers drummed on the cover of his book. 'Was it wise to send her with the parcel?'

'What else? Janice is an American by

birth even though she is of mixed descent, and, to the World Council, above suspicion. Had you or I taken the parcel someone may have noted the incident and remembered it at a later date. Senators and their personal aides do not act as beasts of burden. To do so would have been to act out of routine, and at all costs we must avoid suspicion. Janice, a mere office employee, would not have aroused comment.'

Nagati remained silent. It had been he who, while Sucamari remained in the public eye at Hainan, had travelled a hundred uncomfortable miles to pick up the package. Who had left it where he found it, he didn't know. How many lives had been lost in preparing it he didn't think about. The Orient was vast and the World Police couldn't be everywhere. Experiments could be conducted and men die and be disposed of without an automatic investigation. Not as in the Occident, where the police were everywhere, andall research was confined to approved laboratories regularly inspected.

But he did know that the secret laboratory had been obliterated and all trace of the effort needed to produce what the box contained lost forever. Even the scientists who had bred the bacteria were probably dead and disposed of. The Samurai who had acted in the matter were as fanatical in their way as Sucamari in his. Death, their own or that of others, was not important against the greater threat.

For there must be no question of retaliation against the Orient. 'We shall check,' said Sucamari. 'You will phone from a public booth outside.' He donned his smile and led the way from the legation.

★   ★   ★

Sucamari lived in the old Japanese Consulate on 5th Avenue, not too far from the World Council Buildings and, if a man didn't mind crowds, a pleasant enough walk. Sucamari didn't like crowds, not the noisy, jostling, ill-mannered crowds found in the Occident. He demanded transport at the controller's desk and waited patiently for a turbine car to come from the garage to drive him

114

home. Nagati, declining the offer of transport, decided to walk.

He broke his journey at two different videophone booths, but even so arrived at the Consnlate at the same time as the senator.

'Janice did not deliver the parcel,' he said when they were alone in the study. 'The Asian Antique shop have not received it.'

'Have you contacted her?'

'I tried to. She has not returned to her lodgings.' Nagati paced the carpeted floor. 'I don't like this,' he said. 'She was ordered to deliver the parcel and has not done so.' He halted and stared at the senator. 'Could she have been a spy?'

'For whom? Rayburn?' Sucamari looked thoughtful. 'It is possible, of course; all things are possible, but I doubt it. Rayburn has spies, that we know, but I should say Janice is not one of them.' He sat motionless, staring before him. 'We must find her. Phone her again.'

'From here?'

'Yes. If she answers mention some trivial matter. Hurry!' His tension betrayed

115

itself by a thin film of moisture on his forehead. He wiped at it, annoyed with himself for the betrayal. He must remain calm. He must stand outside events and watch them, taking no emotional part so that, by his attitude, he could control the things affecting others. He was a chess player moving pawns and remaining unaffected by their loss. Nagati cut the connection and shook his head.

'She isn't at her lodgings.'

'I see.' An Occidental would have sworn. Sucamari did not swear. He rose to his feet. 'We must trace her, and quickly. Get the car.'

'In the city?' Nagati had had some experience of traffic conditions. 'Wouldn't a cab be better?'

'No.' Sucamari didn't bother to explain why. He waited until the aide had left the room and, from a rosewood cabinet, took a needle gun. It was more a work of art than a practical weapon, but it held a clip of twenty darts, each no more than a millimetre thick, and each dart was tipped with an anaesthetic paste. One dart would knock a big man groggy, more would render him unconscious, ten would be fatal.

Sucamari slipped the weapon into his pocket and went outside to where the car waited with Nagati at the wheel.

Janice lived on the edge of Chinatown, sharing a bachelor room with another Eurasian girl. It was a pleasant enough room with printed curtains and lacquered prints on the walls. Nagati, interviewing Janice's room mate, first spoke in his native tongue then switched to English when he saw that she didn't understand.

'Pardon the intrusion,' he said politely. 'You are Pearl?'

'That's me, brother.' Pearl was a thorough American despite her slanted eyes and saffron skin. 'You know me?'

'Janice has often spoken of you.' Nagati hesitated. 'It is important that I find Janice, and quickly. A matter connected with some urgent work, you understand. Where would she be?'

'No idea.' Pearl lit a cigarette. 'She didn't come home, that's for sure. Maybe she had a date with her boyfriend.'

'You have his address?'

'No, but I've got his vid number. Janice was always calling him and she wrote the number on the wall.' She pointed to a pencilled scrawl. 'See? Even got a heart drawn around it.' She clucked her tongue against her teeth. 'Poor Janice, she sure has it bad.'

'Phone the number and see if she is there,' ordered Nagati. 'If she is not, then find out where she could be, the address and any other information.' He smiled to take the sharpness from his words. 'The matter is urgent,' he explained. 'I would not like to see Janice lose her employment.'

'Like that, is it?' Pearl took the money Nagati offered her, raised her eyebrows at the sum, and ran downstairs to the video-phone.

When she returned her face was flaming. 'Lousy bitch! The landlady, I mean, she . . . ' Pearl broke off. 'Never mind. I guess I can stand that sort of talk for Janice.' She held out a scrap of paper. 'I wrote down the address. Janice isn't there. Her boyfriend's name is Baylis; he's a messenger at the World Council, but he isn't home, either.'

'Thank you.' Nagati hurried back to the car and gave Sucamari the information. The senator stared thoughtfully through the windscreen.

'A messenger,' he said softly. 'I wonder?'

'Rayburn?' Nagati had followed the other's train of thought. 'Someone making up to Janice so as to spy on us?'

'Emotions are unpredictable,' reminded Sucamari. 'How would Rayburn know that his agent would appeal to our little office worker?' He beat his hand softly against his knee. 'What great emotion would have made Janice forget her duties? Love? Perhaps, and not a smooth passion but an uneasy one. Either she has taken the parcel with her to some rendezvous intending to deliver it later or she has given it to someone else to deliver. Baylis? Perhaps. Or perhaps she opened it and . . . '

'The value was not high,' interrupted Nagati. 'Hardly sufficient to tempt a thief.'

'A person in love is not logical,'

reminded Sucamari. 'It is possible that Janice needed money desperately. And you are wrong about the value of the parcel. Here in the Occident there are many collectors of antiques who would pay a large sum for such an item.' He came to a decision. 'We will call on this Baylis.'

★　★　★

Baylis lived in a cubicle in a human rabbit warren. Fancy clothes, scattered toilet articles, a big tv set and a store of empty bottles showed the way his money went. Nagati wrinkled his nose at the scent of masculine perfume, his eyes sharp as he stared around the cubicle.

'You a cop?' The landlady, a big, blousy female with straggling hair and pig eyes, licked her lips with anticipation. 'What's he done this time?'

'It's a personal matter,' said Nagati. 'I am trying to locate a young lady; maybe you have met her? A Eurasian, a person of mixed blood,' he explained. 'A pretty girl with slanted eyes.'

'The Chinese, I know her. The woman bobbed her head. 'You her old man?'

'No, just a friend.'

'Tough on you then,' she sniggered. 'Real gone on wonder boy she is. Keeps phoning and getting real desperate.' She laughed with coarse humour. 'Don't need much to guess why.'

'Has she been here? This evening?'

'No. She called though and wonder boy dressed up and went out somewhere. Guess they've got things to talk about.' She wiped the back of her fleshy hand across her mouth. 'But if he thinks that he can bring her back here after they're married, if they get married, he's got another think coming. I don't want my lodgers upset by arguing couples and whining kids. I run a respectable house I do, and I'm going to keep it that way. So . . .'

'I understand,' said Nagati quickly. He stared at the big Perbox standing in one corner. 'Would you have a master key to that?'

'To his box?' She looked offended. 'Say, what sort of a woman do you think I am?

121

A snooper? Let me tell you, mister, there's never been a complaint yet about the way I run my house.'

'I'm sure there hasn't.' Nagati pulled out his wallet and showed her a large denomination bill. 'It would be worth this to me just for one look inside that box,' he hinted. 'And your silence about my visit, naturally.' The note crackled between his fingers. 'Now, if you should happen to have a master key?'

She did. She simply jammed her thumb against the lock and pulled open the door.

'Some folks are dumb,' she snickered. 'I slipped a couple-plate in this box when he first came; one print for him, one for me. Funny how some so-called smart guys never seem to think of that.'

Nagati couldn't blame the absent Baylis for not thinking about it. Changing the locks on the standard Perboxes without damaging the manufacturer's seal wasn't easy. The landlady, obviously, had had help. He glanced at the specifications on the lock; it was a single. A couple-plate shouldn't have fitted it. The change had cost money and was illegal. Why the woman had done it he couldn't guess. Curiosity, perhaps. Some people will do anything to satisfy their curiosity. Nagati shrugged; it was none of his business. Neither, as it turned out, were the contents of the box.

Sucamari heard the news in silence.

'We've got to get it back,' said Nagati. 'What if I went to the police and reported the theft of a parcel, describing the contents as that of the one Janice is supposed to have delivered?'

'To do that would be to start an investigation we cannot afford.' Sucamari half-closed his eyes as he leaned back in his seat. 'The whole point is that we dare not admit ownership of the parcel and what it contains.'

'Why not?' Nagati was troubled. 'It is perfectly safe as it is. The statue, even, can be handled without fear. No one needs to know what the coating contains.'

'You underestimate the Health Army and the World Police.' Sucamari was abrupt; he had already thought all this out a dozen times before. 'The culture, I admit, is dormant and will only spring to life when in contact with the right medium, such as blood or natural saliva. But that isn't the point. Secrecy in this matter is our only safeguard. To go to the police is to throwaway that safeguard.'

'Then what shall we do?'

'We wait. Eventually we shall contact Janice and discover what she did with the parcel. At the same time I will circulate my interest in Oriental works of art among the dealers in the city. If it has been stolen we may recover it that way.' He gave a short laugh.

'Strange, Nagati, how even the best laid plans can be upset by a trifle. A girl who is desperately in love forgets her duties and the work of fifteen years is threatened with oblivion. It almost makes you believe in fate.'

Nagati didn't answer; he wasn't superstitious.

8

Rayburn's dilemma

Doctor James Armridge was a tall, slender man with a mane of thick white hair and a pair of firm yet gentle hands. He checked the reading on the portable electrocardiograph, jotted down his findings, then removed the electrodes from Rayburn's torso.

'That's all, Jack. You can get dressed now.'

'How am I doing?' Rayburn, big, stocky, his barrel chest covered with a thick mat of hair, paused as he zipped his shirt. 'How long have I got?'

'That depends.' Armridge pursed his lips in the age-old manner of medical men who are asked more than they consider they should tell. 'I wish that you'd come down to the hospital for a thorough check-up. There are some laboratory tests I'd like to make with 'non-portable equipment.'

'Quit stalling, Jim.' Rayburn spoke with the familiarity of an old friend. 'How long can I keep going without ruining my chances?'

'Not long.' Armridge put away his instruments, fitting them neatly into their lined cases. He didn't look at the senator.

'This is serious, Jim.' Rayburn adjusted his jacket, selected a cigar from a box on his desk, lit it and inhaled with slow deliberation. 'I want to know how long I've got. Five years? Ten? How long?'

'I can't tell you that.' Armridge snapped shut the final case. 'No doctor can. You can't measure life with a clock, Jack, there are too many variables. Your heart isn't as sound as it should be for a man of your age, and your arteries are showing signs of progressive hardening. Catabolism has accelerated and your reflexes aren't anything to be proud of. You're an old man, Jack.'

'I know that. I've lived a long time. Now, how about answering my question?'

'You haven't got ten years, Jack. Maybe five, but certainly not ten. My advice is that you make preparations to take the treatment during the next six months.'

'Are you talking as a doctor or as a friend?'

'Both.' Armridge settled himself in his chair. 'Let's face it, Jack, you're no longer young. You've been driving yourself too hard and now you've got to pay for it. You may last another few years, but if you do, it will be because dope is keeping you alive. The treatment is good, but not that good. Take it in time and you've nothing to worry about; leave it too late and you won't be able to assimilate the serum. It will kill you.'

'It may do that, anyway,' said Rayburn. 'At the best I've only forty-nine chances out of fifty.'

'The two percent death rate?' Armridge shrugged. 'Percentages can mean what you want them to mean. You think that out of every hundred people applying for the treatment two fail to make it. Right?'

'What else?'

'You're forgetting the age groups. From forty to fifty, providing health is good, there is no death rate. From fifty to sixty, again if health is good, it is about one tenth of one percent. From sixty to seventy there is a jump to an average of one per cent. Over seventy things begin to get out of hand. Most of it has to do with the actual physical age, not the chronological age. A man can be young in body even though he has lived a long time, and, of course, you can get the reverse.'

'So the longer a man waits the less his chances of coming through alive?'

'Yes.' Armridge lifted his hand. 'Now, before you start blowing your top, let me tell you a couple of things. We haven't publicised this for the obvious reason that we don't want every forty-year-old demanding the treatment. A man is in his prime at forty and he's got a family to raise before he can think of retiring. On the other hand, we do tell all those who are getting near the danger point that it's time they made their arrangements. Most of them ignore the recommendation. That's where you get your two percent death rate from.'

'Are you trying to frighten me, Jim?'

'I'm telling you the facts.' Armridge

was curt. 'As a friend, I'd like to see you survive the treatment; as a doctor, it would be best if you didn't. We've too many people as it is,' he explained. 'Medical science and antibiotics have kept people alive who normally would have died. Add to that the stoppage of natural death and you've got a headache.'

'I know it,' said Rayburn. 'Blue should have had more sense. He should have used his discretion.'

'That old argument?' Armridge shrugged. 'Personally, I can't think of anything worse than living in a society ruled by immortal despots. Blue knew what he was doing. The great pity is that he died when he took his own serum. He was an old man, physically old, and it killed him.' He stared at Rayburn. 'The same as it will kill you if you wait too long.'

Rayburn sighed and stared at the tip of his cigar. Logically, a man would be a fool to wait too long, but since when have men been logical? And what man, ever, has consciously accepted the fact that he must die? There was simply too much to do before a man could take the treatment.

The majority had no choice; they had to keep working as long as they could, both in order to provide for others and for themselves. A man stayed in the commercial rat race as long as he could to store wealth against the time he must accept legal death. Himself?

'We've known each other a long time, Jim,' he said quietly. 'I respect you as a doctor and appreciate you as a friend. But I can't take your advice. There is still too much for me to do before I drop out of the picture.'

'Politics?' Armridge was contemptuous. 'It's a disease, Jack, as much a disease as cancer used to be. The lust for power grips you. The desire to beat the other man, to be the big fish in the pond. But, when you look at it, what's it all about? A hundred years from now things will be just the same, one faction striving to get the edge on the other, men shifting their loyalties from one party to the next.' He shook his head. 'Take my advice, get out while you're safe.'

'Quit? And then what?' Rayburn dragged at his cigar. 'To spend the rest of my life in a Restezee Home? To watch while fools make a mess of the world? Or perhaps I could scratch around and sell my political knowledge to the man who will take my place? No thanks!' Sparks flew as he ground the cigar to ruin.

'Take it easy, Jack,' said Armridge softly. 'It comes to us all.'

'Does it?' Rayburn was bitter. 'No, Jim, you're wrong. It's easy for you to talk. What have you to lose by taking the treatment? All right, so you'll be declared legally dead, but what does that mean to you? You'll lose your right to vote, to own property, your present situation. You'll make a will and your heirs will inherit just as if you had really died. But when you come to it, what will you really lose? Not your skill, the very thing that has given you all you own. Not your knowledge; you'll still have a trade and the right to practice it anywhere in the world. Knowledge, Jim, that's your safeguard. But what have I got?'

'Complaining, Jack?'

'You can call it that. I've made my life and I don't regret it. I'm not whining at the regulations, but I am complaining because those regulations rob the country of the experience it needs.' Impatience overpowered him and he rose, pacing the floor with jerky strides, his entire body a quivering dynamo of restlessness. 'Damn it, Jim! There's still so much to be done.'

'Relax, Jack, you're beating your head against a wall.' Armridge smiled at his friend. 'Why don't you accept the inevitable? You're not poor and can make arrangements to spend your life in comfort. I know that you've set your heart on power, but you can't keep it for always. The people won't allow it.'

'The people!' Rayburn paused in his striding and sat down at his desk. 'The people, Jim, are sheep. They follow the man with the loud voice and believe that he is doing what they want him to do instead of the reverse. People, in the mass, are fools.'

'Because they don't want to restore nationalism? I'm not an old man, Jack, but I'm capable of a long-term view just the same. Every generation breeds some-one like you; someone with the gift of rousing the rabble, a man who sincerely believes that he has a great mission in the world, and who honestly thinks that he is the only man with the right answers. Such men are dangerous. They are the prime cause of war.'

'So I'm a warmonger,' said Rayburn. 'Is that why you advised me to take the treatment?'

'In a way, yes.'

'So it appears that I can no longer rely on your medical advice.'

'You wouldn't rely on it anyway.' Armridge wasn't annoyed. 'You'd be a fool if you did. You've probably been checked by other physicians before you sent for me, and the betting is that at least one of them was a Blue. Am I correct?'

Rayburn remained silent.

'You don't have to answer,' chuckled Armridge. 'Only a man both stupid and poor would pick a young medico when he could go to a man with a century of experience behind him.' He chuckled again. 'Thanks for the patronage, anyway.'

'Age does not automatically bring wisdom,' said Rayburn, but didn't believe it even as he said it. He lit a fresh cigar. 'What is your picture of the political field?'

'Your part in it? On the face of it you are trying to win a following among our own people by appealing to their patriotism, shrewdly pointing out the taxes we are paying for the immediate benefit of the Orient and using all the old tricks of tub-thumping, semantic phraseology and the rest. The reason?' Armridge looked thoughtful. 'Aside from winning popular support for its own sake, I can only assume that, if you demand secession from the World Council, your following will be large enough to force the motion through.' He chuckled at the concept then, as he stared at Rayburn, grew serious.

'Secession,' he said. 'But why? Because you want to be a bigger fish in a smaller pond? Or because you want to get everything neatly tied up before you take the treatment?' He shook his head. 'No point in that. Once you take it you automatically finish with politics. Unless?' He sat upright, his eyes startled. 'If we secede from the Council,' he said slowly. 'And if you could force through a motion to restore civil liberties to the Blues, then you wouldn't have to lose your power. You'd be firm in the saddle, an immortal at the head of government. Is that it, Jack?'

Rayburn didn't answer.

'It fits,' said Armridge wonderingly. 'By God, it fits! A dictatorship with you at the head. Rayburn, you fool! Do you know what you're doing?'

'Doing?' Rayburn smiled through the smoke of his cigar. 'Aren't you jumping to a few extreme conclusions, Jim?'

'Yes, I guess I am.' Armridge sounded relieved. 'It wouldn't work anyway; you'd be pushing against too much dead weight. People aren't willing to follow a man who threatens their immortality.'

'There would be no threat,' said Rayburn. 'Assuming that you're right, of course. The people would stand to gain, not lose.'

'You'd be offering nationalism and a to-hell-with-the-rest philosophy which would ruin us if we tried to enforce it.' Armridge was very emphatic. 'Damn it, Jack, don't you know how much we are envied as it is? We still have some living space and the natural resources and technology to make the most of it. We could get by and let the rest of the world go their own merry way to hell, but we daren't do it. Envy could so easily turn into hate and, if we secede, we'd wake up one fine day with bombs on our doorstep. And don't mention the World Police; they wouldn't be able to stop it, not if the rest of the world ganged up on us.' He stared seriously at the senator. 'Don't try it, Jack. Secession would only mean trouble.'

'You think I could?' Rayburn was eager. 'Do you really think I could?'

'No.' Armridge relaxed. 'Of course you couldn't. Conditions aren't right for talk of secession, anyway.' He chuckled. 'Speculations like that can sometimes get out of hand.' He glanced at his watch. 'It's late! I've got to get moving.' He rose to his feet. 'Now take my advice, Jack, and don't leave it too late.'

★ ★ ★

After the doctor had gone Rayburn sat alone in his study and stared before him. He lived in what was almost a relic, an unconverted house on the edge of what had, a long time ago, been a fashionable part of the town. Now it was an oasis of privacy in a quarter where privacy was almost unknown. He was thinking of the doctor and what he had said.

He had been right, too right for comfort, and Rayburn felt a brief panic at the thought that he could be so transparent. It had taken years of careful jockeying to reach his present position, but the goal was worth the effort. Immortality and eternal power! It was the old dream of every petty ruler and king through the whole history brought up to date. And it was possible, so possible that it was almost reality. But he needed a little more time before he could blossom into the acknowledged saviour of his country. Once he did that, the rest would follow.

Rayburn sat back in his chair feeling the frustration he knew so well. Intangibles, the hints of hidden purposes, that so swiftly resolved themselves into noth-ingness. And how could he confide to anyone the motivating force of his ambition? What, for example, would Armridge have said had he told him that he feared a monstrous plot by the Orient against the Occident, and especially against the Americas? The doctor would have laughed and said that the senator was justifying his desire for power. Or he would have scorned the concept and demanded proof.

And Rayburn had no proof.

Not unless statistics were proof.

Not unless the barely-veiled envy he had seen so often in the eyes of men he had talked with in the Asian countries could be called proof. Not unless full credence was given to his own, intangible fears. And yet, when it came to it, what did he have to fear?

A creeping line on a graph. A population index that mounted and mounted and showed no signs of ever leaving the rising curve. All countries could show such a figure, but where for years the Occident had practised some measure of birth control, the Orient no longer did. They had started with the bulk of the world's population and they had increased their lead. They were a dead weight against modern progress with their adherence to their old ways of life.

Rayburn sighed, his head spinning with figures as it always did when he concentrated on the problem. In less than seventy years the Occidental population lad doubled, then, when it was obvious that someone would have to support the legally dead Blues, it had risen again. Now it was treble what it had been a hundred years ago. In fifty years time?

Rayburn didn't know, but on one thing he was certain. Food was already a problem and the position was getting worse all the time. Already there had been cases of actual starvation and tremendous numbers of people in the Orient were living at a subsistence level. He had never underestimated the survival instinct and, to him, it was the clearest logic that a starving man will try and get food. And if a man, then why not a nation? Sooner or later the peace maintained by the World

Police would crumple in desperate scramble for living space.

And of all nations the Americas were the most fortunately situated, the most glittering prize. Rayburn knew that the time was coming when, to survive at all, they must hit first, hit hard, and make the first blow the last. If they did not, then they would fall beneath the might of the Orient.

A strong man could save the Americas, and Rayburn felt himself to be that man. He would gain eternal power, yes, but he had no choice. First the power, then the safeguarding of his nation. It was the only way and, when the people realised the truth, they would thank him.

But time was running out.

Rayburn felt panic as he thought about it. If he were to gain power, then he would have to act fast. But before he could act he needed proof. He had to have something, some grain of undeniable fact, so that he could demand an investigation and prove to the public that they were in actual physical danger from the Orient. Then, when they were aroused, he would demand secession and they would agree. From then it was but a step to total power with the Blue vote restored and solidly behind him. Then the elimination of potential danger and . . .

For a moment he sat, engrossed in his dreams, then reality dragged him back to Earth. Armridge had warned him that his time was running out. If the dream was ever to become more than a dream he must act without further loss of time.

But he had to have proof.

9

Unknown bacteria

The policeman who had been with Augustine when he had collapsed had worn gloves and had only touched his clothing. The interns in the ambulance, the nurses and doctors at the hospital had followed normal aseptic procedures in that everyone in contact with the patient had worn skin-gloves, a transparent flexible plastic which was sprayed on and dissolved off in an antiseptic solution vibrated with bacteria-destroying ultrasonic and irradiated with ultra violet. The doctors conducting the autopsy had worn the regulation cover-skins. It was, as Jelks said, the most fantastic good luck.

'If anyone else had touched him or attended to him we'd have been in real trouble.' His face on the videophone screen was expressive. 'As it is I've got three nurses, the ambulance staff, the cop, two doctors and myself in quarantine. Fortunately, I made my own lab tests and I think that we've got it under control.'

'So it was disease, not natural heart trouble.' Sam felt invisible hands grip his stomach as he thought about it. 'What is the disease?'

'I don't know.' Jelks shrugged at Sam's expression. 'It's a new one on me, Sam. All I can tell you is that Augustine's blood was full of a bacteria foreign to his normal metabolism. I can't give it a name and I don't know just what it may do. The only certain thing is that it causes coagulation of the blood. My guess is that it does it by increasing the thrombin content, but it could be by some other means. I'm still working on it.'

'How soon will you know?'

'Give me time, Sam. The human body isn't what I would call a simple mechanism.'

'Sorry, of course you're working as fast as you can. Anything I can do?'

'I don't think so. I've got all the help I can use.' Jelks sucked in his cheeks.

'There are a couple of things I can tell you. Examination of Augustine's body revealed a small cut on the ball of his left thumb. It was a fresh wound, probably done just before he collapsed. Experiments with the bacteria show that, when starved, it becomes dormant and then will explode into life when in contact with blood. Human blood, incidentally, not animal. It also shows signs of being anaerobic.'

'Anaerobic.' Sam breathed a sigh of relief. 'That's some help.'

'You think so?' Jelks wasn't so pleased. 'Admittedly, the bacteria can't live in the presence of free oxygen, but don't underestimate it on that account. We had a hard enough job stamping out other anaerobic bacteria that plagued us for centuries. And this particular culture is tough. Once active it can be transmitted by skin intact and oral assimilation. Moisture from the mouth and even perspiration can transmit it.' He took a deep breath. 'Fortunately Augustine collapsed in the presence of the police, but we can't know how long he was infected, or how many people he may have contacted.'

'What is the incubation period?' Sam asked the important question.

'Pretty quick. Rough tests have own that a single bacteria, once in direct contact with human blood, will multiply fast enough to cause fatal clotting within twenty-four hours.'

'Then Augustine needn't have had the disease for that long. If he was infected with a big dose, via that cut on his thumb, he would have collapsed long before twenty-four hour period.' He stared at the image of Jelks. 'Am I talking sense?'

'Yes. If a large colony of the bacteria were introduced directly in the bloodstream and then the subject had some violent exercise, the resultant blood clot would be swiftly carried to the heart. A small clot would pass, but a larger one would kill.' Jelks tried to rub his chin, then cursed as the cover-skin he was wearing prevented the gesture. 'Damn these things. I'll be glad when I can take it off.'

'When will that be?'

'If I'm not dead in another couple of hours, then I won't die at all.' Jelks grinned through the paper-thin, impermeable plastic. 'The trouble is that I can't smoke, and when you've been cooped up in one of these things for over twenty-four hours, brother, you need a smoke.' He became serious. 'It adds up at that. The small clots would cause pain and bring collapse. The hospital here had diagnosed thrombosis before I arrived, that's why they bypassed the heart with an exciter. Normally, that, coupled with the filtering of the blood, would have done the trick. The trouble was that the blood turned almost solid; we just couldn't filter it fast enough. We tried plasma and whole blood transfusions, but that only delayed the inevitable. You can't wash a human body free of bacteria.'

'So, from what you know about it, Augustine need only have been infected a short while before his collapse. Is that correct?'

'That's about it.' Jelks looked shrewd. 'What's on your mind, Sam?'

'Nothing much, just kicking odd

thoughts around.' He smiled at the doctor. 'Let me know when you have more information.'

'I will, if you'll do the same.' Jelks hesitated. 'I sent a medhyp over to the Augustines,' he said. 'No need to let them suffer the pain of grief. Hope that you don't mind?'

'Why should I mind?' Sam felt guilty at not having thought of it himself. 'Thanks, anyway. Bill me for the service, not the family.'

'It's on the house.' Jelks became thoughtful. 'Nice looking girl, Carmen.'

'Very nice.' Sam changed the subject. 'Don't forget to call when you get anything.' He cut the connection and stared thoughtfully at the blank screen.

★   ★   ★

The fear hadn't left him; if anything it had increased. He was thinking of twenty million people crammed into a city designed for only a third of that number. Overcrowding meant unsanitary conditions and close personal contact. If disease was loose in the city then everything was in its favour for rapid dissemination.

The control of disease was the task of the Health Army under Colonel Lanridge, and they would know what to do. Notification from the hospital would have been automatic and already the mobile units would be standing by ready to rush to any point to enforce quarantine. There was really nothing for Sam to worry about and, officially, nothing for him to do. Yet he had the nagging conviction that the problem was more his concern than that of the doctors.

He looked up as Mike called to him from the intercom.

'Senator Rayburn is on his way to see you, sir.' The secretary did not seem unduly impressed by the prospect of a personal visit from the big man. 'He'll be here within a few minutes.' Sam nodded and was working at some papers when Rayburn entered the office. The senator came directly to the object of his visit.

'I have been informed that one of our

messengers died under suspicious circumstances,' he said abruptly. 'I want to know the results of your investigations.'

'Do you?' Sam offered the senator a chair. 'May I ask the reason for your interest?'

It was a fair question, but one which Rayburn couldn't honestly answer. Augustine had been Rayburn's paid spy though the messenger hadn't known for whom he had worked. There was nothing strange in that. Rayburn had, over the years, built up his own intelligence service with extensions into every department he considered of importance. Anything even remotely connected with the Orient was, to him, important. He sought refuge in telling, not all the truth, but in a part of it.

'My interest has to do with the common weal.' Rayburn sat on the proffered chair. He was perspiring and his breathing was ragged. He looked, Sam thought, a sick man. Politely, he waited for the senator to elaborate. 'I think that he was murdered,' said Rayburn. 'I think that he was killed by the enemies of our nation.'

'Do we have enemies?'

'You know what I mean,' snapped Rayburn. 'And I'll thank you not to bandy words with me. I demand that you make the fullest possible investigation into the death of this unfortunate man and that I be notified as to the results of your investigation.' He paused for breath. 'I need hardly remind you that, as the representative of the Mid-Western Americas, I am in a position to demand your co-operation in this matter.'

'I am aware of your position,' said Sam quietly. 'There is no need for you to make demands.' He did not remind the senator of the fact that the World Police, like the Civil Service of some countries, was independent of the Council itself. Senators came and went, but the basic organisation remained unchanged. Rayburn could storm and rave, but he was powerless to alter that organisation. Only a full session of the Council could do that. But he was entitled to make his request.

'I can give you what information I have,' said Sam carefully. 'Augustine was

150

directed by his controller to report to the Australian legation. He exchanged duties with another messenger named Baylis, who had been ordered to the Japanese legation. We can assume that he reported to that legation. He then left the building carrying a parcel. I saw him myself. That was the last time I saw him.'

'The parcel.' Rayburn was quick to pounce. 'Was it from the Japanese legation?'

'Apparently not. They deny any knowledge of it.'

'Check it.'

'I already have.'

'Check it again.'

Rayburn was not to be put off. Sam reached for the phone. The senator stayed to one side, out of range of the scanners, and stared at the screen. It blurred then cleared as Nagati's image resolved itself in full colour.

'Yes?'

'Sorry to trouble you again, sir,' said Sam. 'But it's about this Augustine business. There is a question about the parcel he was carrying when he left the building. We know that he was supposed to report to your legation, and it is reasonable to assume that he was sent on an errand by someone connected with you. Could you clarify the matter?'

'I'm afraid not.' Nagati's smile was artificial. 'I have told you all this before, captain. Neither Senator Sucamari nor myself have any knowledge of the matter.'

'But your staff?' Sam was insistent. 'Have you questioned them?'

'I have. All deny either seeing this man or having sent for him.'

'I see. Thank you.' Sam cut the connection and recalled the switchboard. 'Get me Courier Control.' He waited. 'About that call from the Japanese legation. That's right, the one which Baylis should have answered but didn't. Can you remember who sent it? A girl? Did you know her? Yes, I know you told me all this before, but I want to make sure. She was a member of the legation staff. She had contacted you many times before. Thank you.' The screen flickered into blankness as Sam looked at Rayburn.

'They're lying,' said the senator. 'The Nips are lying.'

'Someone's lying,' admitted Sam. 'But Nagati could have been telling the truth. The person, whoever it is, could have sent for a messenger without his knowledge and now be afraid to admit it.' He frowned at the videophone. 'It's odd though. People who send parcels usually like to know that they have been delivered. Augustine had a parcel, I saw it, but apparently he got it from thin air and it's vanished into the same place.'

'His receipt book,' suggested Rayburn. 'Does that help?'

'He hadn't filled it in.'

'Then they must be lying, and they wouldn't do that without a reason. Those damn Nips killed him!'

'Steady.' Sam was surprised at the other's vehemence. 'It's odd, I'll admit, but there's not the slightest suspicion that they would either want to kill him, or did so.'

'That's your opinion.' Rayburn heaved himself to his feet. Unlike the captain, he had a shrewd idea as to why Augustine could have been murdered. In the intricate game of spy and counter-spy,

153

agents are considered expendable. If Augustine had stumbled on something important and dangerous to the Orient, then his death was logical. Rayburn gritted his teeth at the thought that perhaps he had missed obtaining the proof he so badly needed by so small a margin. His only hope now was that a thorough investigation would reveal it.

'I know what I think,' he said heavily, 'and I won't rest until I find out the truth. That man was murdered and I want to know just how and why.' He paused by the door. 'I expect quick results, captain. The future of our country may depend on it.'

There was silence for a while after he had left the office, then Mike, forgetful of the respect he should have had but hadn't, snorted his contempt.

'Old fool! He's got enemies on the brain.'

'He's lived a long time,' said Sam quietly. Mike flushed beneath the reproof.

'Sorry, sir, but he is a little stupid.'

'To whom? To us, maybe. To himself? I doubt it. Rayburn is sincere and, even if we don't agree with his conclusions, we

154

must respect his sincerity.' Sam rose to his feet and brushed down his tunic. 'But you're right in one thing — he'll give us no rest until we've cleared up the mystery. Hold the fort. If you want me I'll be down in Personnel, then at the Japanese legation.'

★ ★ ★

Personnel held the records of all who had worked or did work for the World Council. It was a large place and would have been larger fit hadn't been for the computers which took care of the records. Sam wrote out an authorisation, waited until a girl took it to the appropriate authority, then had to explain himself to that individual in person.

'I want a file of all employees of the Japanese legation, with photographs. Official business, and hurry.'

While waiting for the computers to scan the files, select the wanted records and copy them, together with photographs, Sam called through to courier control.

155

'I want you to stand by on this line,' he ordered. 'I'm going to show you some photographs and I want you to pick the one of the girl who sent for Augustine, Baylis rather. Understand?'

The man did. His memory was good and his job had developed his memory for faces. He identified Janice without hesitation. 'That's the one.'

'Are you certain as to that? Certain enough to swear to it?'

'I'm certain.' The man was curious and would have asked questions, but Sam cut the connection. He had no time for idle curiosity; he had questions to ask of his own.

Nagati received him with strained politeness.

'Really, captain, while we all know you have your duties to attend to, isn't this getting rather monotonous? Three times now I have answered your questions. Should I write them all down together with the answers?' He was ironic, but Sam didn't let it bother him.

'The pursuit of knowledge is the asking of many questions,' he said. He held out the file he had obtained from Personnel. 'I would like to speak with this young lady.'

'Janice?' Nagati glanced sharply at the captain. 'May I ask why?'

'You may. From information received I have reason to believe that this person is the one who summoned the dead messenger. If you will call her, please?'

'But this is ridiculous!' Nagati gestured with his hands. 'What possible connection can she have had with the unfortunate death of that man?'

'Probably none,' admitted Sam. 'But police work is the gathering of many details. Most of them are quite irrelevant, some fit into the general pattern, a few are essential, but all are important in that they fill in the general picture.'

'But surely you do not go to all this trouble every time a man dies from natural causes?' Nagati was genuinely amazed.

'Augustine did not die from natural causes,' said Sam evenly. 'The girl, if you please.'

'I am sorry, but you cannot see her.'

'Cannot?' Sam raised his eyebrows. He had battled with diplomatic privilege before. 'May I remind you that the girl is a national and does not come under the protection of your legation?' He did not add that, where the World Police were concerned, there was no such thing as diplomatic privilege.

'Please do not misunderstand me, captain.' Nagati was all apologies. 'I would be only too pleased to summon her, but, unfortunately, she is not here.' He gestured again with his hands. 'She did not report for work today, or yesterday. When she does she will be dismissed.'

'I see.' Sam frowned for a moment in thought. 'Have you any idea where she could be found?'

'None.'

'Thank you.' Arguing, Sam knew, was waste of time. The aide was either lying or telling the truth. In either case he would have to find the girl by normal police methods.

★ ★ ★

Nagati, after the captain had gone, stood a long moment before entering the inner office. Sucamari glanced sharply at his aide.

'Something wrong?'

'The police were enquiring about Janice. The captain wants to find her.'

'I see.' Sucamari toyed with a scrap of carved jade that he used as a paperweight. 'Will he find her?'

'No.' Nagati didn't elaborate, and Sucamari was glad that he didn't. Both he and the aide knew that there was only one sure way of stopping a person's mouth, but he was civilized enough not to want to think about it. Nagati wasn't thinking of the girl; he had other news. 'The messenger who took the parcel did not die of natural causes,' he said. 'The police captain was careless and told me so.'

'Careless, indifferent, or shrewd?' Sucamari never made the mistake of under-estimating his enemies. 'Not that it matters. Without proof his suspicions, if any, are harmless to us. How did the messenger die?'

'Rumour has it that he collapsed from

heart failure.' Nagati looked grim. 'Now we know that he did not die from natural causes. It could not have been accidental. The man was a spy, probably working for Rayburn, and he must have opened the parcel. There is no other way to account for his death and the interest of the police.'

'If he contracted the disease, and we aren't sure yet that he did, then he must have broken the outer seal of the culture.' Sucamari rose from his desk and stared out of the window. Before him the terraced buildings of the city reared towards the sky. He stood there for a long time before turning back to the office.

'There is nothing we can do now but wait,' he said. 'I have already spread word among the dealers that I am interested in ivory Buddhas in inlaid boxes. There is nothing more we can do.'

He moved towards the door as the recall signal chimed for his presence in the assembly chamber.

10

The Mariguana Group

Gerald Waterman leaned back in his seat and wished that it wasn't impolite to yawn. Despite the air conditioning, the assembly chamber seemed stuffy, or perhaps it was the psychological effect of listening to too many boring speeches. Even Rayburn seemed subdued, and the visitors in the public gallery, tourists mostly, had nothing to arouse their interest but the spectacle of one senator after another rising to say what he or she had to say about the Calcutta project.

The reporters were frankly bored. In their section, half-filled with the monitoring panels of the newsfax cameras scattered throughout the chamber, they smoked and dozed and furtively played poker. The concentric rows of senators, their aides, secretaries and various officials of the World Council, sat and smoked, or doodled, or leaned back with closed eyes, perhaps deep in concentration or most likely asleep. A few wore headphones, but the majority did not.

Gerald breathed deeply, hoping to kill his desire to yawn by oxygenating his blood, then reached for his headphones, turning the switch to English. The phones remained silent, naturally; there was little point in the interpreters translating the senator's own language. Gerald turned the switch to French, a language with which he was familiar, then relaxed as the smoothly-modulated voice of a female interpreter murmured in his ears.

'. . . I say that this proposal should not be passed without due and serious consideration from each and every member of the Council. I am not one to stand in the path of progress — my record on that score can speak for itself, but I do feel that it would be wrong, criminally wrong, to rush in and grant this fantastic expenditure before every angle and facet of the project has been thoroughly discussed. I can only repeat, as I have done so often, that no nation, or group of nations, no matter how big their hearts and how generous their inclinations can . . . '

Gerald switched off the headphones. Trust Rayburn to hog the last few minutes, even though he was only using his mouth to make empty sounds. The Calcutta project would be adjourned until the next session when it would, if Gerald knew his politics, be passed by an overwhelming majority. Rayburn was only delaying the inevitable.

The assembly broke up and Gerald approached Rayburn to remind him that he was now on leave. The senator, as usual, proved awkward. He stared at his aide as though he had uttered an obscenity.

'Leave? But you can't take leave. Hell, man, don't you realise the work we have to do before the next meeting?'

'It's all taken care of, senator,' soothed Gerald. 'And you did give me permission to visit my father at this time. It was just after we returned from Hainan,' he reminded. 'Now I've made all the arrangements.'

'Then I suppose you'll have to go.' Rayburn grumbled, but inwardly he was pleased. Gerald had a habit of being around at the most awkward times, and there were certain things he wanted to attend to. 'Don't be too long,' he warned. 'We've a battle before us and I want to be ready for it.'

Gerald nodded and moved away, eager to break off the conversation. Rayburn and his battles! Personally, Gerald was sick of the senator and all his manoeuvrings. A blind man could see that Rayburn, at times, was beating his head against a wall with his nationalistic drum beating. The Calcutta project would go through and nothing Rayburn could do would stop it. His protests merely reflected on the area he represented and made the other diplomats regard him more as a figure of fun than an adversary to be reckoned with.

Gerald, despite his education, was, in some ways, very ignorant of the ways of men. He didn't stop to think, for example, that the more Rayburn was held in contempt by the other senators, the more solid would be his support from his own area. Most men have a weak spot for the underdog, and the conservative farming element would be all for a man who talked down-to-earth, money-saving politics. Rayburn wasn't concerned with his reputation in the assembly chamber half as much as he was with his reputation among those who had voted him into power.

* * *

A cab took the aide to the air terminal, its turbine whining as it edged along in low gear through the central traffic, only gaining real speed when it reached the raised highways. At Teterboro Airport Gerald caught the express jet to Jackonsville, Florida, dozing for most of the two-hour journey. At Jackonsville he had a ninety-minute wait; his chartered jetcopter was due for an engine replacement. To kill time he went for a walk along the coast.

He didn't like what he saw. The sea was calm enough, the rolling, slate-grey waves coming in from the Atlantic and surging against the piles and breakwaters, but the strip along the coast was devoted to the sea farms and the drying of harvested kelp. Men, mostly Blues, worked at the drying racks, turning the redolent seaweed with long-handled forks, baling the dried weed and man-handling it to the pick-up stages.

The stench of drying kelp and rotting fish was heavy on the air. Sea workers, fishermen, longshoremen and a scattering of undersea farmers and contract labourers on shore leave thronged the boardwalks and jostled obvious strangers. They were a rough, hard bunch. Men who lived dangerously and acted it. Gerald, in his neat clothing, very conscious of his soft hands and soft muscles, was glad to get back to the safety of the airport.

In the restaurant he had a meal, a good one, consisting of various kinds of fish and molluscs, took his time over his coffee and unashamedly listened to a couple of spearfishers arguing the merits of their equipment. One favoured the old-fashioned pressure gun while the other was all for the new rocket harpoon. From what Gerald could make out neither had much advantage over the other. An attendant signalled to him just as the argument showed signs of developing into a fight.

At the desk he attended to final details.

'Thumbprint this, and this, and this.' The clerk held out a series of forms. 'Thank you, sir. Are you certain that you don't require a pilot?'

'No pilot,' said Gerald. 'My licence is in order and I want to handle the machine myself.'

'Just as you wish.' The clerk's opinion of amateurs was obvious. 'If you get into trouble just press the panic button and leave the rest to the machine and to us. In that eventuality you'll have to pay the cost of the rescue party plus any damage you may have caused.'

'Even in the event of mechanical failure?'

'Mechanical failure excepted.' The clerk spoke of that remote possibility as an atheist would refer to the Day of

Judgment. 'You're fitted with a trace-signal, so radio in if extending time of hire. If you don't we'll come after you.' He grinned. 'You pay for that, too.'

'Maybe it would be cheaper just to buy the machine?' suggested Gerald.

'That, or hire a pilot,' agreed the clerk. 'No? Well, it's your funeral. Good luck and pleasant flying.'

★ ★ ★

From Jacksonville to the island of Mariguana in the Bahamas took a slow and easy three hours with the jetcopter, set on automatic, doing most of the work. Gerald took over for the last fifty miles, made a slight course correction and arrived just as the sun was sinking below the western horizon.

Despite the fading light, he made a perfect landing before a long, low, solidly-built house facing the shore. An attendant, still wearing his daytime clothing of big hat and coveralls, came from an outhouse and took charge of the machine. Without speaking to him,

Gerald made his way into the house. A receptionist smiled at him from behind a counter.

'May I be of assistance, sir?' He, like the outside attendant, was a Blue.

'Mr. Waterman,' said Gerald. 'My father is expecting me.'

'Yes, sir.' The receptionist gestured towards two heavily-built men who had risen from their seats when Gerald had entered. Despite their telltale pallor, they looked tough enough to handle a bull gorilla. They sat down at the receptionist's gesture and took up their magazines. Gerald wasn't surprised to find that even the bouncers were Blues. Everyone resident on the island was a Blue.

'Mr. Gerald Waterman?' The receptionist did things with an intercom.

'That's right.'

'Thank you, sir.' There was more buzzing and clicking from beneath the counter. 'Did you have an enjoyable trip, sir?'

'Not bad.' Gerald didn't want to make idle conversation, then realised that this man, like almost everyone else on the island, was cut off from actual contact with the outside and was naturally eager to talk. 'Looks as if a storm is gathering about two hundred miles to the West,' he said. 'But I expect you'll get warning if it heads this way.'

'I expect so, sir, we always do.' The intercom hummed. 'Number nineteen, Mr. Waterman. Straight down the corridor.'

'Thank you, I know the way.' Gerald strode down the familiar passage and into a familiar room. His father, looking even younger than he had a year ago, and much younger than when he had taken the treatment, rose from an easy chair and held out his hand.

'Gerald, my boy! Good to see you!'

'And you, father.' Gerald dutifully shook hands. 'How's grandfather?'

'He's fine. Just fine. Everyone is fine.' His father laughed, the laugh of a young, healthy man. 'Sit down and chat a while. The others are in conference, something special, but you'll hear all about it tomorrow. New York the same as ever?'

'The same, only more crowded.'

Gerald glanced around his father's comfortable room, with its books, the fifty-inch television set, computerized music centre and tasteful paintings, the thick carpets and other evidences of luxury. His sighed, remembering his own room back in Rayburn's oldfashioned house, the strain and rush of normal living and the general rat-race of an overcrowded world. To him, at this moment, his father's room seemed a virtual paradise. He said as much.

'Getting tired, Gerald?' His father reached for a decanter, poured golden liquid into a glass and poised it beneath a syphon. 'Say when.'

'When.' Gratefully, Gerald accepted the drink and rolled the smooth Scotch around his tongue. 'Tired?' He shrugged. 'I guess I am a little at that. Sometimes I get the craving just to run away from the whole sorry mess.' He finished his drink. 'I'll get over it.'

'You'll have to.' George Waterman took his son's glass and replenished it. 'Your time for rest will come, Gerald, but not yet. When it does, you may regret it and long for the old days.'

'Not me.'

'No? I think you will, but never mind that. Before you can relax you've work to do and things to see to. Still single, of course?'

'Naturally.'

'Preston's grand-daughter is looking for a husband. I've suggested to Preston that you two might make a match of it and he agrees. It's about time you started to raise a family, Gerald; it can be dangerous to leave things too late.'

'Is she fertile?'

'Her medical says so. You are, I know.' George stared thoughtfully at his son. 'I think you'd better have two children, a boy and a girl. We want to keep the family as flexible as we can.'

Gerald nodded. He wasn't surprised or shocked at his private life being settled for him by his father and his father's associates. It was one of the things he had grown up to expect, and felt neither enthusiasm nor distaste at the idea. He rather looked on marriage and the raising of children as another man would regard a visit to the dentist. It was necessary for his own good, and he would be glad when it was over.

'I don't want you to worry too much about this marriage,' said George. He seemed to think it his duty to make things quite clear. 'It needn't interfere with your normal life in any way, and you'll be free of it, anyway, once you take the treatment.' He smiled. 'You know, in certain respects this legal death has its advantages. I respect your mother, Gerald, she made an excellent wife, but the prospect of spending eternity in her company is something I would rather not think about.'

'Do you ever see her?' Gerald sipped at his drink and wished that his father would change the subject. The old man must think that he didn't know the facts of life.

'Didn't she tell you on your last visit?' George chuckled. 'We see each other quite often. We have tea together sometimes and, in fact, we discussed your marriage prospects. One day, after a few decades perhaps, we may even try living together for a short while.' He dismissed his ex-wife as being unimportant. 'The thing is, Gerald, I want you to be quite determined about this marriage. I don't want the trouble Hardwick had with his son when the young fool ran off and married a television star. Luckily, he managed to get the marriage annulled without much difficulty, but it was an unpleasant incident. The boy was almost in the position of having to support a half-dozen irresponsible dependents.'

'He could have denied them,' pointed out Gerald. 'He didn't have to support them.'

'He didn't, but what of his children? Would they have defied their mother?' George shook his head. 'No, Gerald, you stick to the rules and we'll all be safe. It's for your own good, remember.'

Gerald sighed, wishing that his parent didn't think it so necessary to stress the obvious. Of course he would marry carefully with an eye to the future; that was merely self-defence. And of course his selected wife would feel exactly the same as he did about things. They would marry, have their children and each would live their own lives. Love and romance didn't enter into it or, if it did, was kept quite separate from the essential business of rearing an heir.

He rose as the door opened and another man entered the room. Cyril Waterman was a hundred and twenty-five years old and looked no different than his son George. Or it seemed that way until you saw his eyes. They were old eyes, eyes that had seen much of life and intended to see a great deal more. Gerald, whenever he was with the old man, felt a little like a schoolboy confronted with his headmaster.

'Gerald!' Cyril held out his hand. 'Good to see you. Have a nice trip?'

'Not bad.' His father, Gerald remembered, hadn't bothered to ask about his journey. Perhaps age brought politeness, or could it be caution?

'I've told him what we've arranged with Preston,' said George. 'I think two children, Cyril?'

'Which Preston?'

'Why, Quentin, naturally. He's the head of the clan.'

'Then why didn't you say so?' Cyril snorted his contempt. 'What's the good of calling a man by his surname when there could be four generations of them?' He lost his impatience as he looked at Gerald. 'How do you feel about this marriage, Gerald? Or didn't George bother to ask you?'

'I don't mind, Cyril.' Gerald didn't think it strange to address his grandfather by his Christian name. 'I suppose it's all for the best.'

'It is, make no mistake about that.' Cyril gestured about the room. 'You see all this? You'd like to know that exactly the same comfort awaits you when it's your turn to take the treatment, wouldn't you? Then marry wisely and keep the money inside the family.' He clapped Gerald on the shoulder. 'And you can't leave it too late. How old are you? Forty?'

'Thirty-seven.'

'Time you're due to retire your son will be about the right age.'

Cyril nodded. 'Time enough. No sense in marrying too early and saddling yourself with responsibilities before you have to. Just so as your son is mature and knows his duty when you hand over.' He looked at George. 'Two children, you said?'

'I think that would be best,' said George. 'A boy and a girl. You agree?'

'Yes.' Cyril changed the subject. 'How's Rayburn?'

'Mad.'

'Literally, or are you just saying that?'

'Just saying it I suppose, but he seems that way to me at times.'

Gerald stared past his grandfather's shoulder as the door to the conference room swung open. Several men stood inside, all Blues, most smoking and talking quietly together. Gerald had met most of them before on previous visits to the island and he knew them all for members of the Mariguana Group.

One of the men didn't fit into the general pattern. His hair was white but it was a natural whiteness, not the bleached colour of an albino. His lined face and bagged eyes gave him the appearance of an intelligent dog. He turned towards the door and Gerald stared at his familiar features. Cyril, noticing the direction of his stare, turned and smiled.

'Prosper,' he called. 'Come and meet my grandson.'

Numbly Gerald shook hands with the head and owner of the Alpha Project.

11

Sam watches television

Carmen was on the phone when Sam returned from duty at the assembly chamber. The small screen did nothing to detract from her beauty and he noticed, with satisfaction, that she had apparently recovered from her grief. She smiled at him, her teeth very white against the redness of her lips.

'Can you help a girl in need of help, Sam?'

'Name it.'

'I'm stuck with a survey job, just a check, but I could do it a lot faster if I could use your monitoring room. May I?'

'Where are you now?'

'Downstairs in the vestibule.' Her smile grew wider. 'I tried to move through the usual channels but got bogged down in red tape. Then I thought of you.' She became serious. 'If I'm out of line, Sam, just say so.'

'Technically you're out of line,' said Sam, then winked at her image. 'Meet me in the self-serve. I'll be about five minutes.'

'I follow.' She smiled again, then vanished as she cut the connection. Sam turned to Mike.

'Anything come in yet about that missing girl?'

'Janice?' Mike shook his head. 'Not yet. I've sent copies of her file to the local police and they are keeping a check on unidentified bodies. I put a couple of our own men to check on where she lived, her boyfriend, things like that. So far, no luck. She just seems to have vanished. Maybe she wanted to disappear?'

'Maybe.' Sam glanced at his watch. 'Anything from Jelks?'

'No, sir.'

'Did you get the report from the local police about Augustine?'

'They finally sent in a copy.' It was Mike's contention that the local police were deliberately unhelpful to the World

Police. Sam reserved his judgment. Personally, he had no cause for complaint. He picked up the flimsies, scanned the report and then looked thoughtful.

'So he complained that he'd been robbed. He was breathless as if he'd been running and didn't seem to know just what he was doing.' Sam flipped the sheets. It fitted, all of it. If some petty criminal had stolen the parcel that would account for it being missing.

But it still didn't account for Augustine's death. Running should not kill a healthy man, and it certainly wouldn't fill his blood with unknown bacteria. He dropped the report; it had told him little he did not already know.

'Do you think that Rayburn could have something on the ball, captain?' Mike had obviously given the matter some thought. 'If Augustine was sent for and then slipped a shot of dope, wouldn't that account for it?'

'You've been reading too many thrillers,' said Sam. 'They sent for a messenger, but they couldn't know which one would answer the summons. And why would they want to kill him, anyway?' He left Mike thinking about it.

⋆ ⋆ ⋆

Carmen was sitting at a table in the self-serve, looking even more feminine than ever against the sterile plastic of the tables and chairs. She waved at him and Sam walked directly towards her, his uniform getting him past the guard who watched for non-customers trying to reach the tables.

'Good to see you again, Sam.'

'Again?' He glanced at his watch. 'Seven minutes.'

'I mean in the flesh.' She stared at him with disturbing frankness. False modesty, along with many other conventions, had vanished during the past hundred years. Sam spoke before she could pursue the subject obviously on her mind.

'How are your folks?'

'Well enough.' She shook her head. 'It's funny. I know father died only a short while ago, but it seems as if he's been dead for ages. I suppose I should feel all hurt and tearful, but I don't. Do all people feel this way about death, Sam?'

They didn't, as Sam could have told her. He remembered his own sorrow when his parents had died in a rocket plane crash in the Rockies. But then, all people didn't have the services of a medical hypnotist to dull reality. The medhyp had both removed the memory of his visit and taken the emotional charge from her recent memories. Such therapy was fast becoming standard practice now that death had a new meaning.

To cover his failure to answer her question he produced cigarettes, offered her one and lit them both. Carmen inhaled, let smoke stream through her nostrils and frowned down at the table.

'Mario's talking of emigrating,' she said abruptly.

'Emigrating?' Sam was startled. 'Where would he emigrate to?'

'I don't know. He just keeps talking about getting away from it all, stuff like that. Sometimes it gets me worried.'

'He must be thinking of taking a job on

one of the government developments,' said Sam. 'The Antarctic mines can always use volunteers. That, or he's just plain forgetful. He must know that no nation now permits emigration unless it's on an exchange basis.' He didn't mention that the Antarctic mines were used as a penal colony for law-breaking Blues, or that there was an obvious interpretation of the remark. The only way for Mario to 'get away from it all' was by suicide. He reverted to the object of her visit. 'So you want to use our monitors, do you?'

'I'd like to, if I could.' She remembered her coffee, rapidly growing cold, and drank it before continuing. 'It's the Miracle Maid account. They want us to check their flashad programme. You know how we operate. A section of the public is exposed to the advertising and then we check the increased sales in that area.'

'Just like that? The increased sales, I mean?'

'Near enough. People always buy after being subjected to the flashads, and the rise in sales is predictable to within five per cent. The trouble is that the increase in this area wasn't as high as it should have been and Miracle Maid want us to check to see that they haven't been gypped.'

'Nice people.' Sam was amused. 'Don't they trust anyone?'

'In the advertising game you can't trust your own mother,' said Carmen seriously. 'And I mean that literally. Flashad time on the tv circuits is strictly limited by your people, and the contents of the advertisements are censored. That's why you monitor the tv services. Static installations and mobile projectors are more flexible but they don't reach as wide a section of the public and they aren't as effective. For really predictable results you need the tv screens and tri-dis; most viewers are practically hypnotised by them, anyway.' She crushed out her cigarette. 'So if you could help me, Sam?'

'As a visitor to the building, it is a part of my job to show you around. Strictly off the record, naturally.' He smiled and glanced at his watch. 'I'll just tell the office where to find me and then we can get going.'

'Thanks, Sam.' Carmen was grateful. 'But if it means trouble for you, don't bother.'

There was no trouble. The monitoring room was staffed with bored and cynical operatives who were only too happy to break their eternal routine of examining slowed-down recordings of tv transmissions. To check them all was impossible unless they increased their staff by a factor of ten, but every broadcast was recorded and spot checks made to see that no one broke the regulations governing flash advertising.

Carmen told the file clerk what she wanted, received a recording and joined Sam at a viewer.

'Get what you wanted?' Sam had diplomatically stayed in the background while the staff had basked in their visitor's beauty.

'Yes, thanks. The Miracle Maid account ran with the Spot Quiz at that period.' Deftly she fitted the recording into the viewer. 'This is saving me a lot of time, Sam. The alternative would have been to go to the studios, get pushed around by every clerk in the place and then probably wind up with an edited copy.'

'Then why don't the advertisers make their own recordings?' Sam drew a couple of chairs before the screen and rested the control panel on the arm of Carmen's chair. 'You know how to operate this?'

'I think so.' She checked the controls. 'Yes, I can. They're the same on most commercial viewers. Did you ask why the advertisers didn't make their own recordings?'

'I did.'

'Can you guess how many advertisements are put out by each big company every day, Sam? Twenty-four hours a day, don't forget, and scores of channels on the tv circuits alone. Couple that with printed advertisements, whisper-speakers, static and mobile flashads, videophone transmissions and the rest of the merry-go-round and you'll get an idea of the problem. To record and file everything would take a place as big as this.' Carmen threw a switch that lit the screen. 'Anyway, why duplicate? That's what this place is for.'

'Then why come to me?'

'Because I could only get a copy of this recording by filling in goodness knows how many forms and waiting until Doomsday for my turn on the list. And Miracle Maid want the answer now.'

'So you used your influence with a certain member of the World Police to bypass the normal channels and so build up your reputation with your firm as a girl who can get things done. Is that it?'

'That's about it.' She turned and smiled at him, her face alluring in the glow from the screen. 'Mad at me, Sam?'

'How could I be?' Sam fought the desire to take her in his arms.

'Let's get on with the show.'

He had seen slowed-down recordings before and had watched the monitors at work, but even so he had to admire Carmen's skilful handling of the controls.

She ran the recording at high speed and then slowed it as she came to the part she wanted.

'Recognise it?'

'I think so.' Sam stared at the screen. 'Isn't this the programme we watched on the day your father died?'

'Yes.' Her laugh was a little tremulous. 'I haven't bought any Miracle Maid products since then but I guess that I wasn't a very receptive subject at the time.'

She adjusted the controls. 'The ads were scheduled for one every minute, on the minute.' The screen flickered and blurred as she increased the speed, then halted with a blaze of colour at exactly the right spot.

'Nice, isn't it?' Carmen made a face at the crude design of the flashad. 'Maybe that's why we weren't affected; these things are aimed strictly at morons.' More pictures glided over the screen. 'Slightly different, but still crude.'

She sighed as she ran the film to the next advertisement. 'You know, Sam, with all the inherent power of this sub-threshold advertising, you'd think that they would be used for something better than just making people buy what they can't afford.'

'It comes under freedom of speech,' said Sam. 'Once you censor what people say and print and sell, and how they sell it, then you've lost your freedom.'

'Meaning that there is no censorship?'

'No, but it's confined to banning things and products which are harmful to the common weal.'

'I see.' Carmen looked thoughtful. 'And just who decides just what is, and is not, harmful?'

'All right.' Sam admitted defeat. 'So we do have censorship. I'm not defending it, because I can't. To me, any form of dictatorship is indefensible, and no one should have the right to determine what others should, or should not, see, read, buy or experience. But, bad as censorship is, I'd rather have it than the so-called good taste of your advertisers.' He gestured towards the screen. 'Do you know that a statistician once worked out the fact that popular entertainment was the greatest single cause of the general lowering of intelligence?'

'What axe did he have to grind?' Carmen was cynical. 'I'm no statistician, but I'll bet that I could make out just as good a case for blaming the stratoliners for the weather, or for the fashion of wearing brilliant clothing being the cause of myopia. Statistics can prove anything you want them to. Surely, you know that?'

'Maybe, but there are some things you can't get away from. Surely you don't advocate free licence on the flashads?'

'They could be worse,' said Carmen. 'After all, your censorship is a hit and miss affair, and it's even money that quite a few firms and studios are breaking the code.' She busied herself with the controls. 'Look, Sam, purely visual.'

'What's the idea?' Sam stared with interest at the image of a smiling female. She was superbly shaped and quite nude.

'Psychologists have proved that the unclothed human body, even in this day and age, has a strange fascination,' explained Carmen. 'This image is to trigger the male response on a subconscious level. Naked woman equals Miracle Maid products, and a consumer will think of one when he is reminded of the other. Male figures do the same for female viewers.'

'Pornography.' Sam was disgusted.

'How low can we get?'

'Quite a bit,' she said seriously.

'And those figures are artistic, not pornographic. Anyway, didn't the courts once rule that what a person can't consciously see couldn't be indecent?'

'A decision which was reversed after the sex riots fifty years ago,' reminded Sam. 'That was when they incorporated the flashed code. Viewers may not have been able to consciously see the images, but they certainly had an effect. Obviously, if they didn't then they wouldn't be used for advertising.' He repeated his first comment. 'I still say that such advertising is pornographic.'

'No more so than using the secondary female sexual attributes to appeal to the eye. The female bust has sold more goods than anything else in history. Read your advertising history if you don't believe me. Why, it was the advertisements which did more than anything else to set the plastic cosmeticians up in business.' Carmen triggered the switch again. 'There! I thought so!'

'What's wrong?'

'This.' The screen flickered and clarified. An advertisement flashed on the screen. It was not the same as the others he had seen. Carmen re-wound the film, raced it through, checked it and said something unladylike. 'So that's their game.'

'I don't get it.' Sam was puzzled. 'Why the excitement?'

'Conflicting advertisements. Miracle Maid specified one flash per minute, on the minute. They got exactly what they asked for, but the studios were smart and ran another series in between on the half-minute. The two advertisements cancel out.' Carmen fumed. 'Damn them! And there's nothing we can do about it.'

'Can't you sue?'

'Maybe, but I doubt it. The radio people would have covered themselves in some way.' She shrugged. 'Well, I've done my part, the rest is up to the lawyers.'

'Finished?' Sam wasn't interested in the complexities of the advertising war. He stooped forward to rewind the film, then paused, staring at the screen. This particular image showed the contender on the Spot Quiz, straining and sweating as he struggled to find the answer to the final question. The camera had swung back to show him at full length standing beside the Quiz Master.

Sam didn't stare at the plump and smiling face of the Quiz Master, nor at the strained face of the contender; he stared at what the man carried.

Memory is a peculiar thing. Sam had spoken to Augustine and had commented on his burden. He had glanced at it, no more, but now he recalled the exact time and incident. Parcels, like almost everything else, have their own characteristics. Some are large, some small, some square, some poorly wrapped, the list is endless.

The contender was carrying Augustine's parcel.

12

Sam goes hunting

The local police were un-co-operative. It was, as the precinct lieutenant pointed out, none of their business.

'Sure, we'd like to help you, captain,' he said. 'But how can we? Where's the crime? Who is making the complaint? Why should we pull in this Joe Leghorn when he's done nothing wrong?' He gestured around the precinct station. 'Hell, captain, don't you think we're busy enough as it is?'

It was an understatement. The local police were more than just busy; they were run off their feet. Even as Sam had waited for his interview with the lieutenant three chowhounds had been brought in, all of them the worse for wear. The food thieves had tried to rob a hydroponic farm on the edge of town, had shot and killed the manager when discovered and had tried to run. Their car had crashed a few blocks away after a running gunfight in which three pedestrians had been injured. The police didn't treat them gently.

On a bench, four people waited to swear out complaints regarding theft. A big man had been charged with mayhem against a Blue; he had beaten up his grandfather-in-law, and sat joking with the sergeant in charge. A group of sullen teenagers had been arrested while on a Blue-baiting, and a corner-prophet waited his turn to be charged with using language calculated to disturb the peace. From a wall speaker the relayed radio instructions to the prowl cars made a continuous background of noise.

The lieutenant sighed as he listened to the speaker. 'Work, work, work,' he grumbled. 'Nothing but work. You guys in the World Police don't know how lucky you are. How the hell do they expect us to keep order in this town? We couldn't do it with twice the men. I tell you, captain, it's like living in a nightmare. If it wasn't for the officers using their discretion we'd be swamped.'

The 'discretion' used by the officers was simple. Petty criminals were beaten up with plastic billys and warned to keep their noses clean. Blue-trouble was usually ignored. Who wanted to worry about the legally dead? Petty theft was booked and then forgotten; a man should look after his own property. Most of the law breakers booked in at the station were fined or, if they had no money, put on probation which, in turn, meant a going over in the back room.

The police weren't sadists, but there was simply no alternative. The courts were flooded and the prisons filled to capacity, so short sentences had been discarded in favour of the unofficial and legally unrecognised punishment dealt out by the officers.

Sam realized that he was wasting his time.

'Have you tried Leghorn's address?' The lieutenant was trying to be helpful. 'Asked among his friends, at his office, the people he lives with? Hell, captain, you know the procedure as well as I do.'

'I've tried all that,' said Sam. 'No luck. They clam up when I ask the questions.'

'They would.' The lieutenant nodded as if he'd expected no different. 'Sorry I can't spare any men to dig him out for you, but you see how it is.'

'I understand,' said Sam. 'Thanks, anyway.'

'If it was official it would be different,' said the lieutenant. 'We always like to help.' He looked thoughtful. 'Tell you what, you might try Father Rosen. He runs a mission down that way, soup and bread for the starving, you know the kind of thing. He might be able to finger this character for you.'

'Thanks, I'll try him.' Sam walked from the station to a public videophone and called his office. Mike's image flashed on the screen.

'Any luck?'

'No.'

'I knew it.' The secretary looked disgusted. 'These local cops have no time for the World Police. Did they tell you to mind their business while they took care of their own?'

'No.' Sam didn't want to discuss it. 'Any word on the missing girl yet?'

'Nothing.'

'Keep trying,' said Sam. 'I'm going hunting.' Cutting the connection, he left the booth.

On the street he paused for a moment, oblivious of the passing crowds. It was late and the sky was filled with clouds and darkness. A streak of fire from a transcontinental rocket express drew a line of brilliance from horizon to zenith, adding to the flaring glow of the advertisements covering the tall buildings. It was never dark in the centre of the city; night only served to throw the man-made lighting into greater effect.

A jetcopter, its riding lights looking like colourful stars, hooted as it released a cloud of luminous gas. Sam glanced up at the sound, then turned away at the tell-tale flicker of a flashad. He had no desire to be indoctrinated with the compulsion to buy something he didn't want.

★ ★ ★

Father Rosen was something of a freak in this modern age; he was a man who still had faith. He was old and stooped, and his face had the loose, sagging appearance of a man who should have been fat but wasn't. His cassock was stained and rusty with time and hard usage. His eyes were kind, though shrewd, and his voice betrayed the man of culture.

Sam found him working in a long, mouldering hall half-filled with a clutter of rough tables and benches. Men and women, many of the women carrying young children, lined up for a bowl of soup and a hunk of bread dished out by an idiotic-looking man wearing an assortment of cast-off clothing, a fringe of straggling beard and a vacuous, lop-sided grin.

'What may I do for you, my son?' The priest came towards his uniformed visitor.

'I would like to talk to you, Father. I need your help.'

'Help?' The question hung in the air. 'A private matter, my son?'

'Yes. If I could speak with you alone?'

'Of course. A moment while I remind

William that, while there are many to feed, there is little to feed them with.'

Sam glanced around the mission as the priest whispered to his helper and wondered just what it was that gave a man the strength to work and live among such abject poverty, apparently, of his own free will. Orthodox religion in the Western nations had lost its influence long before Blue had discovered his magic serum and, now that men no longer had to fear hell-fire, had almost vanished from the scheme of things. Even so, a few devoted men and women still carried on the work of Mother Church and found in the teachings of Christ their own reward.

The priest returned, shaking his head. 'A willing helper,' he said, 'but at times his mind wanders and he forgets what he does. But he has faith, and twice a day he hopes that the miracle of the loaves and the fishes will repeat itself. Perhaps, if he has sufficient faith, it will.'

'Perhaps,' said Sam. 'But isn't it true that God helps those who help themselves?'

'You are a cynic,' said the priest mildly. 'And yet, in this day and age most men are cynics. Even so, it was promised that the meek should inherit the Earth.' He led the way to a small room at the back of the mission. A crucifix hung against one wall, together with a few cheap reproductions of religious paintings. A statue of Our Lady stood on a shelf flanked by candles in ornate holders. A heavy, well-thumbed rosary lay beside a leather-bound missal on a small table. In one corner was a narrow cot. The priest drew chairs from where they stood against the wall, offered one to Sam and seated himself. 'And now, my son?'

'I am looking for a man,' said Sam, coming directly to the point. 'His name is Joe Leghorn, a trouble-shooter living in this area. I understand that you could help me locate him.'

'You are a policeman.' It was not a question.

'World Police, not local,'

'But still an officer of the law. I am a man of God, my son, not of law.'

'You quoted the Bible,' said Sam. 'May

I do the same? 'Render unto Caesar the things that are Caesar's.' But I am not asking you to help me hunt down a man for punishment. I merely want to find him so as to speak with him.'

'And your reason?'

'I am trying to protect the common weal. I have reason to believe that Joe Leghorn has something in his possession that could endanger the city. He doesn't know what it is that he has. I want to warn him and eliminate the danger.' It was, realised Sam, the truth. His subconscious must have been busy adding two and two and arriving at the inevitable four.

The priest stared thoughtfully at Sam. 'You quoted the Bible,' he said abruptly. 'Have you studied it?'

'I have read it,' said Sam. 'Not quite the same thing, I'm afraid.'

'No,' said Father Rosen. 'It is not the same thing at all.' He fell silent, his eyes thoughtful as they stared at the crucifix, then rose to his feet. 'Pardon me for a moment. I must make sure that William does not become too generous.' He left the room and was gone several minutes. When he returned he resumed the conversation as if there had been no interruption. 'To have read the Word of God is something rare in these times, my son. I commend your action even though I may not sanction it.'

'Because of the danger that each man may make his own interpretation?' Sam knew of the Roman Catholic ban on casual reading of the Bible.

'History has proved that the danger is by no means unreal,' reminded the priest. 'But enough of theology. You understand, my son, that my position here is a delicate one?'

'I understand.'

'Men and women come to me and I give them what I can.' The priest sighed. 'It is not easy to see so many have so little. But they trust me, and the poor souls gain some comfort by unburdening their hearts. All, you understand, beneath the seal of the Confessional.'

'I am not asking you to break that seal, Father.'

'I would not if you did,' said the priest

sternly. 'But we digress.'

'I think not,' said Sam evenly. 'You are telling me, in your own way, that you value the trust these people place in you. You feed them, yes, but you try to do more. You try to spread the Gospel among them as those like you have done for more than two thousand years.' He drew a deep breath. 'You will not lose that trust because of me, Father. I am not asking you to turn into a police informer or run the risk of being taken for one. But would you believe me if I told you that I consider the finding of Joe Leghorn of greater importance than your work?'

'Nothing can be more important than bringing souls into the House of God,' corrected the priest. 'But though young, you are shrewd. What makes you think that I can obtain the information you require?'

'Simple. Most of your — parishioners — are Blues. There are a great many Blues in this neighbourhood and they see and hear almost everything that goes on. They have a common bond; those in misery always have a common bond, and they trust and respect you. Their information, because of that, is at your disposal. You have, though you may not know it, a highly efficient intelligence service.' Sam corrected himself with a smile. 'But, of course, you know it. You are an intelligent man.'

'I have been called something other than intelligent at times.'

'Because of this?' Sam leaned forward and touched the back of the other's left hand. It was unmarked. 'Why haven't you taken the treatment, Father? Is it the cost? You could easily borrow the money against a five-year labour contract in an undersea farm.'

'It is not the cost.'

'Then why not take the treatment?'

'Must I live a lie? Can I preach what I preach and yet have so little faith? Life, my son is but a preparation for the world to come. Did not . . . ' He broke off controlling himself as the half-wit opened the door. He stared furtively at Sam, scuttled towards the priest and whispered in his ear.

'Thank you.' Father Rosen pressed the

half-wit's arm. 'Return to your duties.' He stared at Sam. 'The man you seek,' he said quietly, 'is in the shop of a man named Johanasen about six blocks due north from here. You cannot mistake the place. The shop occupies a corner of a warehouse.'

'Thank you.' Sam looked curiously at the priest. 'Why didn't you tell me that you had agreed to help me?'

'Perhaps I had not. It would have been easy for me to have changed my mind. Perhaps many things.' Father Rosen hesitated. 'You understand that I cannot give you a guide?'

'I can find my own way.' Sam rose and then hesitated, staring down at the old man. 'Father, does your religion approve of suicide?'

'It does not.'

'Would you say that a man who, by exercise of free will, deliberately chose to die rather than to live, would be guilty of suicide?'

'A man has his natural term, my son. To extend it is to go against the Will of God.'

'Is it? Then what about all the diabetics who would have died but for insulin? What of the diseased who live now only because of the antibiotics which saved their lives? Did they defy the Will of God?'

'Sophistry,' said the priest. 'Your arguments are not new to me. I know what you are going to say.'

'I am going to say that you have no right to choose death rather than life. Your refusal to take the treatment is tantamount to suicide and directly against the religion you preach.'

'You are wrong.' Father Rosen was not annoyed. 'I believe in the hereafter and the Kingdom of Heaven as revealed to the world by Jesus Christ the Son of God. To believe that, and yet refuse to meet it, is to live a life of hypocrisy.' His thin fingers fumbled for the rosary and caressed the worn beads. 'Eternal life is not for men, but for Angels.'

'Nothing is eternal,' reminded Sam. 'Not on this world, at least; Men still die and still need the truths you teach. Love, kindness, charity. These are the things we need more now than ever before, but those virtues are rare, and those who teach them few. By refusing to live you are robbing the world of something it cannot do without. Take the treatment, Father. Society and your religion both need you.'

The priest did not answer.

'The punishment for suicide is not a pleasant one,' said Sam. 'At least, so you preach. Do you want to spend eternity in Hell?'

'I may go to Hell,' said the priest seriously. 'I am mortal, and mortals are weak. But it will not be because of committing suicide. A Papal Bull has made that very clear. Refusal to take the treatment is not an act of suicide and so is not a mortal sin.' He smiled and, suddenly, Sam felt very young. 'The man you seek may not remain in one place long.' The hint was plain.

'I understand.' Sam moved towards the door. 'Goodnight, Father, and thank you.'

'Go in peace, my son.'

It was benediction and goodbye. The old priest would cling to his faith and, with his dying, the world would lose a little more tolerance, a little more charity, a little more of the spirit of Christ. Sam, as he walked past the long line of men and women waiting for their handout, felt a sudden depression. To him, at the moment, the mission hall seemed a reasonable facsimile of Hell.

Outside, it was raining, a cold, mist-like drizzle which fogged the air and made the streets shine with unaccustomed cleanliness. Above the city hung a red glow of reflected light so that, even here, there was some reminder of the man-made heaven which money could bring.

Sam walked in the middle of the street, acutely conscious of shadowed doorways and narrow-mouthed alleys. He was not alone; no one was ever truly alone on the streets of the city. Eyes watched him from hidden corners and from the humped shapes of homeless Blues huddled together for mutual warmth, too poor even to be able to afford the price of a bed in a communal flophouse.

Johanasen's place was, as the priest had said, on a corner, part of a rambling warehouse which looked as if a high wind would reduce it to rubble. A single door opened on the street and was flanked by a window covered to chest height by gummy brown paint. A stout iron mesh guarded the window against accident. It also guarded the window against cleaning, so that the unpainted upper section was almost as opaque from dirt as the lower part was from paint. A pearly light shining through the grimed glass gave the place a weird, unreal appearance of life.

Sam tried the door, found it locked and kicked on the lower panel. He waited five seconds then tried again, kicking so hard that the door rattled against its frame. Fifteen seconds later he lifted his foot and crashed his heel against the lock. It wasn't a very strong door, but it took a succession of kicks before something yielded with a grate of metal and the door swung open.

'Anyone home?'

Sam stepped from the street into a wide, open space faced opposite the door by a breast-high counter. The light came from a single bulb hanging from a corded flex. The floor was of bare boards. The air was filled with the scent of dust and mildew and, outside the circle of light, shadows clustered as if protesting at his intrusion.

'Can anyone hear me?'

The echoes caught his words, played with them for a little while and then sent them back distorted beyond recognition.

'Joe! Joe Leghorn! Where are you?'

Again the echoes tumbled the words so that they sounded as if the shadows were laughing at some secret knowledge.

Sam frowned and stepped towards the counter, his shoes heavy on the floor. He reached the partition, leaned over it and stared directly down at a crumpled figure in a suit of orange and green.

'Joe!'

Sam jumped the counter and dropped lightly to the other side. He stooped over the limp figure, one hand extended to touch the great artery in the throat, then halted the movement of his arm as he stared towards the edge of the circle of light. Slowly, he straightened and tilted the cone-shaded bulb so that its brilliance illuminated the rear of the room.

A Blue could die the same as any other man from injury or starvation but, unlike normal men, they did not die of disease or illness. Three men and a woman sprawled in the area behind the counter. They were thin, but not starved. Neither bore any sign of injury that Sam could see, and there was no blood. They were all Blues.

And they were all dead.

13

Prosper's Portal

The conference promised to be interesting. Gerald had attended such meetings before, but usually they were a wearisome rehash of the obvious with a constant emphasis on the duties of the younger generation towards their elders. This time promised to be different.

Cyril, at the head of the table, rapped for silence, and, in his best boardroom manner, opened the proceedings.

'For the benefit of late arrivals,' he glanced at Arnold Franks, a man of about Gerald's age, who had only arrived an hour ago, 'I would like to introduce Prosper, of whom you have probably heard. Prosper, you have the floor.'

'Thank you, Mr. Waterman.' Prosper rose to his feet, rested his hands on the table, cleared his throat and began speaking in a dry, almost ironical voice.

Listening to him, Gerald was reminded of a university professor who regarded his students as an unfortunate necessity. He realised why as Prosper warmed to his subject.

'As you all know, or should know if modern methods of news-dissemination are effective, I am interested in interstellar travel. As yet I have received very little support from the public at large, and none at all from the World Council. I am no longer a young man, gentlemen, and so am forced to make a compromise. Mr. Waterman has shown interest in my project and has asked me to tell you something about it.'

'Keep to the point, Prosper,' said Cyril dryly. 'You are not trying to sell us something.'

'I am offering you something which you could not buy,' said Prosper quietly. 'I am offering you a new world.'

'The Alpha Project?' Gerald bit his lips at his grandfather's expression. Damn the old man, anyway; wasn't it bad enough that he had ruled his life from the cradle? Gerald scowled and made doodles on his scratch pad. Money was nice, and security was nice, but sometimes he felt that those things could be bought at too high a price.

'The Alpha Project,' agreed Prosper evenly. He straightened from the table. 'Men have been bound to one solar system for too long,' he said. 'It is time they left the system of their birth and ventured out into the seas of emptiness around us, seas which are filled with islands each of which would double our living space and offer mankind a new home. Eighty-five years ago Shizzy Murphy tried to reach Alpha Centauri in a nuclear-powered spaceship in which he hoped to accelerate to near-light speed and so make the journey in his own lifetime. He used conventional rockets to reach free space, but his ship exploded as soon as he had engaged the nuclear drive. With his failure the dream died. Today, the prospect of interstellar travel is regarded as a joke.'

'Spare us your advertising.' Cyril was frankly bored. 'We are business men and interested only in facts. Please keep to the point.'

'I had not left it.' Prosper's dry voice held a snap. 'Would you rather I went?'

'Don't talk like a fool, man.' Prosper had more spirit than Cyril had given him credit for.

But he didn't alter his tone. The Mariguana group had the money, as Prosper did not, and those with the money always held the power. 'You need us more than we need you,' he reminded. 'Please continue.'

'Very well.' Prosper stared down at the table and fought his rising inclination to walk out. What the chairman had said was true. He did need them and, if his dream was ever to become more than a dream, he would have to yield to them. But it was hard, and if he had been twenty years younger . . .

'Shizzy Murphy was impatient,' he said quietly. 'He couldn't wait for the research then in progress to be perfected. He tried the old method of rocket propulsion, riding mounted above a mass of nuclear material and taking a madman's gamble with death. He lost and his tomb circles the Earth. But in losing he did more than just die — he killed man's dream of reaching the stars.'

'The risk was too great,' said Gerald. He made a point of not looking at the head of the table. 'With immortality at stake men weren't interested in taking such risks.'

'Exactly.' Prosper smiled towards his supporter. 'But when Murphy made his journey, elsewhere scientists were investigating the possibilities of foreshortening space rather than in fighting it with rocket power. In the Americas alone there were four research projects working on the problem. Longevity came, and then the depression. Money was short and the projects were abandoned. But, though abandoned by the government, it was not forgotten by the workers. A small group, beaded by my father, carried on, their private investigations. My father died, killed in a laboratory explosion, but I carried on with the remainder of his fortune and what help I could obtain.' He paused and glanced around the table. 'I was successful.'

'You are telling us that you have

perfected a means of foreshortening space, is that it?' Quentin Preston, his forward-thrusting jaw and heavy jowls giving him the appearance of a pugnacious bulldog, snapped the question.

'I am.'

'Then why haven't you sold it to a transportation company?'

'I am not interested in planetary transportation,' said Prosper mildly. Quentin snorted.

'Then you should be. Sell the invention, and with the money gained build your interstellar Portal. Simple business logic.'

'Perhaps, but it isn't quite as simple as you seem to assume. Seven years ago now, we sent a spaceship on its way to Alpha Centauri. It is now almost four light years from here. It is slowing as it approaches its destination. In a few months it will be in a position to land and establish the Portal. A gateway from Earth to another planet,' Prosper paused, and smiled. 'A direct link. A connection built through space and time, which circumnavigates both. Four light years becomes a single step.'

'A matter transmitter,' said Quentin.

'No,' Prosper said. 'Not that. We do not break down, broadcast and reassemble. I doubt if we shall ever be able to operate in such a manner. We merely extend. Call it a space warp if you like. Space and time have been co-joined so that we are in direct contact with the other end of the link. We shall continue to stay in contact no matter how far way that link is in terms of normal distance. In a few more months, you will be able to step through the Portal on Earth into the ship and from the ship to the surface of a new world. A little later, when the ship has been dismantled, one step will suffice.'

'If you can land,' said Quentin. 'If you have enough power. If — ' He broke off, feeling foolish. 'But those things present no problem.'

'No,' said Prosper. 'We can supply the ship from here. With food, fuel, air, water and crew. We can supply power from installations far too vast ever to be mounted in the hull of any vessel. We have only one real problem.'

'Somewhere to land,' ventured Quentin. 'A world suited to human life.'

'We have already chosen,' said Prosper. 'Spectroscopic analysis has shown us a planet almost identical to Earth. No, that is not the problem.'

'Then?'

'Money,' said Prosper. 'Money to buy power to maintain the link. Money for essential equipment, for supplies, tools, the thousand and one things we shall need if we ever hope to settle a new planet. Money,' he said bitterly. 'That is our only remaining problem.'

'So it's expensive.' Quentin seized on the important factor. 'How expensive?'

'I will need about two billion dollars to pay for the power. It is that which has forced me to beg for funds.'

'Too expensive! Why, with that . . . ' Quentin broke off as Cyril rapped on the table.

'We will reserve discussion until later,' ordered the chairman. 'Thank you, Prosper, that will be all for now. If you will wait in the lounge?' He waited until the old man had left. 'Well, gentlemen, you heard what Prosper had to say. Any comment?'

They all had something to say, Quentin Preston, Jud Franks, Henry Crowder, all the heads, sub-heads and new-Blues of the Mariguana clan group. Only Arnold and Gerald remained silent; Arnold probably out of respect for his elders, Gerald because he had learned from experience that nothing he could have to say would make the slightest difference.

He sat back, intent on his doodling, glancing at the other junior with idle curiosity. Had his wife already been selected for him? Was he married and doing his duty to his clan? Gerald glanced at Quentin, then hurriedly looked away. That bulldog expression! He straightened as Cyril called the meeting to order. 'Let me make it quite clear that we are going to back Prosper and his project,' he said calmly. 'If we don't, then the Ford clan will.' The threat won their attention as he knew it would.

'But two billion!' said Quentin weakly. 'It's fantastic.'

'For what Prosper offers?'

Cyril shook his head. 'I think not. Let us look at the proposition as a long-term investment. By backing Prosper we gain control of his invention and so will have a virtual monopoly of interstellar travel. With that monopoly we can dictate what passengers and goods we carry to our new world. And it will be our world, gentlemen, never forget that. We shall have sovereign rights and can make our own laws. The best and most profitable investment we could ever make.' He drew a deep breath. 'Need I elaborate further?'

Cyril was clever; he didn't state the obvious, but every man in the room knew exactly what he was driving at. On a new world the old laws wouldn't apply. There would be no need for any Blue to suffer legal death. He was offering them a private empire with every advantage a power-hungry man could wish for.

Gerald, sitting back, could see the expressions of the men around him. Their forced retirement to the Mariguana Restezee Home was anathema to them; they wanted the feel of actual authority, the fire and clash of business, the power to tell others what they must do. For a moment he toyed with the idea of cutting free, of liquidating the assets in his name and starting over afresh in some new locality. He could do it, he knew; the law did not recognise the property rights of any Blue. He could defy them all and laugh in their faces, for all they had over him was the power of tradition and so-called duty. But since when has any tyrant or dictator had more?

Gerald knew that he would do exactly as he was told to do. And now he learned the real reason for his presence at the conference.

'Rayburn has some power in the Council and he may be persuaded to use that power on our behalf. It shouldn't be hard to use him to obtain a government grant to help us found the new company.' Cyril had it all worked out. 'That is your job, Gerald. You will persuade Rayburn to iron out all difficulties. You may promise that he will be given a position of authority in the new regime. That should win him over if his record is anything to go by. Further details will be sent to you, but you can start winning Rayburn over to our side without delay. You know what to do.'

Trust the clans to look after themselves, thought Gerald. Always have some of the heirs close to those in authority so that they can use their influence when necessary. Revolt stirred within him, to die as soon as it was born. The elders knew best, trust the elders. He had been conditioned to that all his life.

There was more small talk and then to Gerald's surprise, he was dismissed.

'Best for you to get back,' ordered Cyril. 'We want to get this thing moving without delay. Arnold will attend to the financial details while you work on Rayburn.' Cyril rose to signify that he could leave.

'I'd hoped to stay over until tomorrow,' protested Gerald 'It's getting late, and I won't be able to reach New York until well after dark. Besides, I'd like to visit my mother.'

'Plenty of time for that, son.' George, swollen with self-importance, his head full of the grand prospect of being part-owner of an entire planet, ushered him towards the door. 'You do as Cyril says. Plenty of time for visiting when the job's done.' He chuckled. 'There's a great day coming, boy. A great day.'

Gerald yielded, knowing argument was useless. He glanced at Prosper sitting in the lounge and wondered what the old man was thinking. Probably burning inside at the treatment he had received. He smiled as Prosper looked at him.

'I'm leaving now for New York,' said Gerald. 'Can I give you a lift to Jacksonville?'

'No, thank you. There are still certain details to clarify, and then I am leaving direct for New Mexico. A plane has been chartered.' Prosper returned the smile. 'Thanks all the same.'

⋆   ⋆   ⋆

Aloft in the jetcopter, the controls set on automatic, Gerald stared sourly down at the island. The old men had been smart, he had to admit that. When the legislation had been passed making all Blues legally

226

dead, Cyril and the others had got together and formed a clan group. They had bought the island and built the homes. A limited liability company held all their wealth, the heirs of the clans being hereditary stockholders. Most of the income from the company, together with twenty percent of the earnings of the heirs, went to ensure the comfort of the elders.

They couldn't be blamed. It is natural for a man to want comfort and security; but at times Gerald wished that Blue had never discovered his serum. The tyranny of the undying was, at times, irksome.

At Jacksonville he handed the jetcopter back to the charter firm and booked passage on the north-bound express. He was tired with long travelling, and George had kept him up half the previous night with business and family gossip. He took advantage of the five-hour wait for the express to catch up on his sleep. He booked in at a transient hotel, made sure that the clerk put a fresh plate in the Perbox, registered his thumb-print, transferred his valuables to the safety of the steel vault and went to bed.

He didn't sleep well. Two hours before his plane was due he woke to the sound of shouting in the streets and the noise of heavy trucks rumbling down to the shore. He tried to get back to sleep, failed, rose, showered, dressed, reclaimed his property and went down into the lounge, where be learned the reason for all the noise. One of the undersea farm domes had collapsed killing a hundred men and stranding a hundred and fifty others who had been working outside. They were now trying to make their way to the shore in their suits. The noise was from the rescue parties racing against time and distance in an effort to reach the men before their air gave out. The clerk who relayed the information wasn't optimistic.

'They're twenty miles out on a forty-fathom bottom,' he said. 'It's rough country out there. If we can save ten percent of them it'll be a miracle.'

'Tough,' said Gerald. He was thinking of the labour contracts that would be voided by the actual death of the workers.

'Tough,' agreed the clerk.

228

They weren't thinking of the same thing.

★ ★ ★

The express had a full complement of passengers, most of whom were bound for New York. Gerald found himself sitting next to a plump matron who reeked of lavender and who insisted on telling him all about her Guru; an Indian who was teaching her all about the mysteries of the East at five hundred dollars a lesson.

'He's a simply marvellous man,' she said for the dozenth time. 'Such big, soulful eyes, and so unworldly. Why, you'd never believe it, but I actually had to *force* him to take the money. He just didn't want it; said that everything is Karma — that's illusion, you know, and that money is the biggest illusion of all. And he's *so* understanding. And he's so nice, and very wise, and he's over a hundred years old, and, as I told the girls at the club, that just goes to show because he must have learned a lot having lived so long, and . . . '

Gerald nodded and smiled as if interested, and privately thought that at least one Blue had hit upon a lucrative racket. Though even at five hundred dollars a session it must have been hard work. He should have charged double and so gained at least four times the reputation. His customers, to judge by the matron, obviously belonged to the class who believe that the more expensive a thing is, the better it must be.

At Teterboro there was trouble. A uniformed policeman, local, not World, stood by the barrier checking the new arrivals. The public address system kept repeating over and over that all passengers bound for New York City should report to the administration building. Gerald showed his credentials to the officer and asked the natural question. The policeman was too busy and too tired to argue.

'Ask at the desk, mister, they'll tell you there. Next! Chicago? Over to section eight, follow the red line. Next!'

Gerald left him to it and walked to the

administration building. All other exits from the airport were closed, guarded by more uniformed police. Jetcopters drifted in the sky, their lights flashing the ground-or-else signal. Gerald frowned towards them, reminded, in some way, of the fuss and confusion he had left behind at Jacksonville.

At the administration a harassed clerk told him the reason for the guarded airport and the guarded sky.

New York was in quarantine.

14

The plague spreads

In a room on the eighty-seventh floor of the General Mercy Hospital, Sam Falkirk sat and waited to discover if he was going to live or die. It was a pleasant enough room, with a bed table and chair, television screen, music console, books and magazines, and all the luxury of a high-priced private ward. It was small consolation to know that, if he did die, none of this need be destroyed with him. The cover-skin he was wearing would take care of that. The only things that could pass the paper-thin plastic were sound vibrations, air and light. Sound was transmitted by a stiffened portion that served as a diaphragm, and the plastic was transparent. A valve admitted external air and another fed the respiration through an oxygen trap. If Sam were to die the cover-skin would be used as his coffin.

If he were to die. For the hundredth time he reviewed exactly what had happened when he had found the dead Blues. He had kicked open the door, walked across the floor and had jumped the counter. He had touched the door, the counter and the overhead light. And that was all. But he had breathed the air in the place and had almost touched the body of Joe Leghorn.

Sam was hoping that that 'almost' would save his life.

He had called the Health Army immediately, giving his instructions and then standing guard until the mobile squad had arrived. They had been very efficient as, dressed in their cover-skins, they had collected the dead and sealed the premises. Towards Sam they had been gentle but firm. He had been exposed to the disease. He was suspect. He must be isolated and cleared. Now he waited for the verdict.

He picked up a magazine, glanced at the inflated torso of a tv actress advertising a new brand of soap, put it down and selected another. This time the same actress assured the world that she owed her charm and figure, not to the plastic cosmeticians, which would have been anyone's guess, but to a certain laxative. A third magazine gave the information that laxatives only created internal disorders and that Wondercrack, the bulk food which contains no protein, carbohydrates or vitamins, nothing but good, old fashioned roughage, was the one thing to give good health. It also, according to the pictures, provided a royal road to rapid promotion, wealth and, naturally, the automatic happiness which wealth would bring. Sam had a vivid mental picture of millions of low-income employees religiously eating the stuff and waiting hopefully for the rapid promotion. It had to be rapid. If they ate nothing else they would starve to death before it came. He put down the magazine as Jelks entered the room.

'Relax,' said the doctor. He looked tired and his eyes were red from overstrain. 'You can take that thing off now and have a shower. You're clear.'

'I am?' Sam felt a tremendous relief.

Now, for the first time, he knew how a condemned criminal felt when reprieved at the last minute. His legs suddenly grew weak and he sat on the edge of the bed. Jelks glared at the unrumpled cot.

'Didn't you get any sleep?' He answered his own question. 'Of course you didn't; how the hell could you relax?' He slapped Sam on the shoulder. 'Get that thing off and have a shower. I'll have coffee here by the time you've cleaned up.' He remembered something. 'Here's your uniform. It's been cleaned and irradiated. Hurry now.'

True to his promise, hot coffee stood on the table when Sam returned from the shower. He poured two cups, added plenty of sugar and passed one to Sam.

A package of cigarettes lay beside the tray and he shook a couple free, waited until Sam had inhaled, and then lit his own.

'This is a bad situation, Sam,' he said. 'Have you spoken to Lanridge yet?'

'How could I?' Sam drew at his cigarette with the satisfaction of a smoker who has been denied tobacco when he needed it most. 'The colonel must be as busy as hell and, anyway, I've been cooped up in here since I sent in the warning.' He stretched with animal pleasure. 'It's good to know that I'm not under the chopper.'

'I can guess.' Jelks looked at the tip of his cigarette. 'Lanridge told me that they found twenty dead in that shop, eighteen Blues and two others, one of them the owner. It was lucky you found them when you did.'

'How long before we can start tracing the progress of the disease?'

'We've already started,' said Jelks grimly. 'Johanasen, the owner of that junk shop, ran a soup kitchen and used the rest of the premises as a flop house. The Blues we found dead in his shop worked for him. He must have contaminated everyone around him during the past twenty-four hours of his life.'

'That's the effective period, isn't it?' Sam looked thoughtful. 'I've been in quarantine for that long, so all those Johanasen contaminated must be dead by now.'

'And all those whom they contacted will be dead in the next twenty-four hours and so on.' Jelks didn't look happy. 'How many people do you think a carrier could contaminate in that time, Sam?'

'Plenty.' It didn't require a genius to know that. 'Is the twenty-four-hour period definite?'

'Yes. If a man doesn't die within that time then there was nothing wrong with him in the first place. We've found out a few things since I spoke to you last. About the bacteria, I mean. The death of the Blues threw new light on it. You know that the longevity serum effectively protects the body against all normal bacterial and virus diseases?'

Sam nodded. 'I don't know why though.'

'Neither does anyone for certain. My guess is that the serum alters the metabolism a trifle, not enough so that ordinary food can't be assimilated, but enough to make the body so alien to invading germs that they don't stand a chance.' Jelks gestured with his cigarette. 'Excuse the terminology. I'm too tired to think of the fancy words.'

'I wouldn't understand them if you could,' said Sam. 'One day I'll have saved enough money to afford a hypno-course in preliminary medicine, but that day isn't yet.'

'Save your money,' advised Jelks dryly. 'It takes ten years of actual hospital work as well as the hypno-courses before you can qualify. Even then you're only allowed to empty the bedpans. Patients don't like amateurs working on them when a mistake can cost them immortality.'

'That's understandable.' Sam drank the last of his coffee. 'But I didn't mean that I wanted to become a doctor. Not that it's a bad idea at that; plenty of security in the future.'

'Security means a lot to you doesn't it, Sam?'

'Your coffee's getting cold, why don't you drink it?'

'So you don't want to talk about it.' Jelks shrugged and gulped his coffee. 'I could say a lot about the psychological aspect of that, but I won't. Why should I treat you for free anyway?' He smiled then became serious. 'You're getting on, Sam. When are you going to marry and start raising some kids?'

'Plenty of time for that yet.' Sam changed the subject. 'Lanridge put on a local quarantine, of course?'

'At first he did, but it wasn't any use. Now it's total.'

'Total! The whole city?'

'Didn't you know?' Jenks glanced towards the tv screen. 'Hell, Sam, what have you been doing with yourself all this time?'

'Thinking.' Sam didn't go into details. The thoughts of a man who believes that he may die are something more than private.

'We had a case outside the quarantined area,' said Jelks. 'Lanridge immediately sealed the city and warned everyone to go home and stay there. Then, when that didn't work, he sent out a freeze-or-else.' He shrugged. 'That worked. Or it did after people began to believe that he meant what he said.'

'They would.' Sam was grim. 'Damn it!

To think a few microbes could cause this trouble!'

'A few microbes,' repeated Jelks. He lit a fresh cigarette, apparently forgetting the one he had smouldering in the ash tray. 'They were no accident, Sam.'

'What's that?'

'I said that this disease is no accident.' Jelks met Sam's level stare. 'Those bugs were made to order.'

'Are you sure?' Sam wasn't surprised, not as much as he should have been. He'd had a sneaking suspicion that something was wrong ever since Augustine died. But feelings weren't important against concrete evidence. 'Proof?'

'Only the bacteria itself. It's too close to the perfect germ weapon to be accidental. Look at Anaerobic for easier control. It kills with a hundred percent efficiency. You can't do anything when your blood starts to solidify, except pray. It has a short incubation period and its speed of propagation is fantastic. It's selective in that it is harmless to animal life, and it kills Blues and non-Blues both.'

'And that makes it a weapon?'

'What else? There isn't a natural disease known which has hundred per-cent killing efficiency. Not even the mutated viruses developed during the old cold war had that. They were bad, yes, but everyone had a greater or lesser resistance to them. They were normal diseases in that they entered the body and started a war to the finish. If the virus won, the man died. If the man won, he lived. With this thing, no one stands a chance because there is no fighting. The bacteria simply enters into a relationship with the thrombin and increases its effect by an incredible amount. The clotting of the blood is merely a by-product of that relationship, but it a by-product which kills.'

'A weapon presupposes an enemy,' said Sam slowly. 'If you are right and this thing was hand-made for use as a weapon, then they, whoever the enemy are, wouldn't have released it without having some form of protection. Can you figure out some way of gaining immu-nity?'

'First we've got to find out all about what we're trying to immunise against,' said Jelks. 'At the moment we're concentrating on finding out what this stuff does. When we know that, and a lot more, we can begin to find something to combat it. But that will take time, Sam, lots of time. And there needn't be an anti-toxin at all.'

'Would the enemy, if there is an enemy, have released it without?'

'It depends on who they are,' said Jelks slowly. 'It's early to tell yet, but I've the idea that this thing is pretty short-lived as compared to some diseases we used to have. It can thrive while in the human body or similar medium, but deprived of that medium it will die. Like syphilis, if there aren't any men there can't be any syphilis. We got rid of that pest by treating everybody, and I mean everybody, with a double-effective dose of neopen. The same result would have been achieved if everyone had died.'

'I follow,' said Sam. 'The Americas are surrounded by oceans. With a twenty-four-hour death period from time of infection it would be simple for the enemy to ensure a quarantine period for all travellers from this area. Not that the World Police or Health Army would permit such travel in the first place. So they wait until the thing burns itself out for lack of more hosts. They wait until the dead have decomposed and the danger is past. Then they move in. If there is a 'they,' that is.'

'You doubt it?' Jelks looked distastefully at his cigarette, then threw it into a disposal unit. 'You still think that this is an accident?'

'I don't know.' Sam was thoughtful. 'If this thing is what you claim, then they've released it pretty clumsily. So far, it's just local. If it were a weapon, surely it would be all over the Americas by now?'

'How much proof do you need?' Jelks was irritable with fatigue. 'I tell you that the bug isn't natural. If it was we wouldn't be here now to argue about it. Men can't live with solid blood in their veins.'

'Take it easy,' soothed Sam. 'When did you sleep last?'

'I don't remember. Not since Augustine

died, I think.' Jelks snapped his fingers. 'I forgot. Your girlfriend wants you to phone her. She's stuck at your office and seemed worried about you. I promised that you'd phone as soon as possible.' He gestured towards the videophone. 'Go ahead. You've got crash priority.'

Mike answered the phone, his worried face staring from the screen. 'Sam! Are you all right?'

'Perfect.'

'Are you sure? No . . . ?'

'No bugs, no nothing. No need for you to pass the hat.' Sam smiled at his secretary. 'How are things?'

'It's hell,' said Mike simply. 'Glad you're all right, sir.'

'Not as glad as I am,' said Sam dryly. 'Is Carmen there?'

'Yes.' Mike's face vanished, to be replaced by Carmen's anxious expression.

'Sam, I'm so glad. It was terrible thinking that I might never see you again. Are you sure that there's no danger?'

'I'm sure.' Sam became suddenly aware of Jelks at his side. 'How is it you're at the office?'

'I was in the building when the freeze-or-else order came through, and now I can't move. Mike tells me that if I try to get home I'll be shot down in the street. Is that true?'

'It's true, right enough.' Sam was serious. 'Don't try it, Carmen. The Health Army mean what they say. Everyone has to stay in the building they are in until given permission to leave. Any unauthorised persons on the streets will be shot without question.' He smiled at her to minimise the situation. 'Anyway, what have you to worry about? You're in the best place there is at a time like this.'

'I'd be more comfortable if you were here.' Her smile was rank invitation. 'Coming home, Sam?'

'Home?'

'Home is where your heart is, or didn't you know that?'

'Home is where I hang my hat.' Sam cut the connection and stared at Jelks. 'When can I get out of here? With the city in stasis I'm needed at the office.'

'I've arranged transportation,' said Jelks. 'You'll have to wait until the Health

Army gives you clearance and an escort. If you try it alone you'll be shot down just the same as anyone else. Those boys don't play, Sam, they can't afford to.'

'I know.' Sam stared absently through the window. Below and before him the city, blazing with advertisements, sprawled like one jagged-backed monster, the soaring towers of the new buildings dwarfing the squat bulks of the old. Normally the streets could have been filled with traffic, the sidewalks crowded with pedestrians. Now a strange emptiness had replaced the restless tide of movement, and even the sky was devoid of traffic. Only the drifting jetcopters of the air guards made moving touches of colour against the night sky. Sam shivered a little, despite the warmth of the air-conditioned room, and turned from the window to meet Jelks' stare.

'What made you do that, Sam?'

'Do what? Stare out of the window? Shiver?'

'What made you insult that girl? She's in love with you, don't you know that?'

'So she's in love with me.'

Sam helped himself to another cigarette. 'Must I marry her and raise a parcel of kids just because of that?'

'No,' admitted the doctor.

'But it helps to have a wife who's in love with you — especially when you're in love with your wife.' He rose and stood by the captain. 'What's wrong, Sam? Why can't you and Carmen make a go of it?'

'Isn't this rather an odd time to be talking about love and marriage.' Sam gestured towards the window. 'Personally, I think that's more important.'

'Maybe you're right.' Jelks pressed his fingers against his eyes, blinking as he relieved the pressure. 'But I'd like to know why it is you're afraid of marriage.'

Sam could have told him, but he knew he wouldn't. Marriage didn't scare him — children did. It wasn't that he didn't like children; he was a normal, healthy man, but he wasn't happy about the world they would be born into. The world was overcrowded as it was, and getting worse all the time. If he married Carmen he would be morally bound to support her dependants. That wasn't so bad, and if that were all he wouldn't hesitate. But the children of the marriage would also be saddled with the burden, a dead weight on their lives that would grow worse, not better.

He remembered the students at the school, young, eager, hopeful as all young people should be. None of them realised what they had to face; a lifetime of work, chained to the concept of family duty. The alternative was a lifetime of loneliness, of guilt at having deserted their dependants, of fear of what the future would bring. The immortality that men had craved since the dawn of time would be a curse, not a blessing. Unsupported Blues lived in a financial hell without end and without hope.

It was a heritage that Sam refused to pass on.

15

Martial Law

Carmen was asleep when Sam arrived at his office. She sat at his desk, her head resting on her arms and she looked very young and very lovely. Sam looked down at her, feeling a sudden tenderness for the girl. He glanced at Mike.

'How long?'

'Since just after you phoned.' Mike yawned and lit a cigarette. He was unshaven, his uniform rumpled and his eyes red from fatigue. A phial of wakey pills stood beside a cup containing the dregs of coffee. His desk was littered with report sheets. 'She was almost out on her feet, and I didn't have the heart to wake her up.'

'She can't stay here.' Sam gently moved a coil of black hair from where it had fallen across her face. 'Has anyone fixed up any sleeping accommodation?'

'For the staff, yes, not for the general public.' Mike rose to his feet. 'I doubt if the staff will be using their beds. Would you like me to take her down to the rest room?'

'Please. Any arguments, refer them to me.'

'They won't argue.' Mike stepped forward and picked up the sleeping girl. She stirred a little, mumbled something and threw her arms around the officer's neck, snuggling her head against his shoulder. Mike looked embarrassed, seemed about to say something and then walked quickly from the office. When he returned he was apologetic.

'She must have thought it was you,' he said. 'We'd been talking about you and she was asleep, and everything.'

'Forget it.' Sam had other things to worry about than Mike's idea of what constituted proper conduct. 'Give me the picture.'

'Lanridge took command of all police and health troops when he issued the freeze-or-else order. External units of the Health may have already surrounded the city with troops and mobile weapons. The local police are guarding the barricades, stations, airports and working with the coast guard to seal the harbour. Our men are concentrating on patrolling the air over the city while the Health Army patrol the streets.' Mike ran his fingers through his hair. 'We've got everything more or less under control now.'

'Good. Any urgent messages?'

'Some of the senators have been ringing through. I've managed to persuade them all that they can help most by staying where they are.' Mike yawned again; and picking up the phial of tablets shook a couple into his palm. He put them into his mouth, swallowed, made a face and ran to the water container for a drink. 'Never could swallow tablets dry,' he explained. He snapped his fingers. 'I almost forgot. Colonel Lanridge wants to see you. He asked you to report to him as soon as you arrived.'

From the office Sam took the elevator to the lower levels stepping carefully over the sprawled figures of sleeping men and women who had been trapped in the building. Below ground level the corridors were clear.

Sam left the elevator and walked along the twisting, anti-radiation passage to the operations room of the Health Army.

Colonel Lanridge did not look like the popular conception of a professional soldier. He was small, slightly stooped, almost bald and with eyes which glistened from the contact lenses he wore. His uniform never fitted, and now it looked as if it had been slept in. It hadn't, Sam knew; the colonel wouldn't have slept since the emergency began. Lanridge was standing at the edge of the map section staring thoughtfully at clusters of coloured lights.

'Hello, Sam, pleased to see you.' He spoke as if he begrudged the time needed for pleasantries. 'Jelks told me that you were clear. Nasty experience.'

'I could have done without it.' Sam examined the map. 'How are we doing?'

'Not so good.' Lanridge picked up a pointer and rested it on the map. 'The red lights show where there has been an outbreak of the disease. This one is where you reported the outbreak, the others have come in since then.'

'So many?'

'Too many.' Lanridge sounded grim. 'My guess is that it was spread by the people who ate at Johanasen's soup kitchen.' The pointer moved to a different point on the map. 'The yellow lights are suspect areas. Persons within them could have been in contact with carriers. The green lights show places that, at the moment, we know to be clean. Small families who can account for every member, and who haven't been out, places like that. There aren't many of them.'

'Not enough,' agreed Sam. 'What is your decision concerning the danger areas?'

'We have issued cover-skins to everyone within the locality, together with instructions to strip and don them. At the end of the critical period, I've set it at thirty hours to be on the safe side, the living will be removed, the cover-skins sterilized, and the dead taken care of.'

'How?'

'Napalm,' said Lanridge shortly. 'We've chosen selected sites for lazar houses, and later we'll burn them and the dead to ash.' He shrugged at Sam's expression. 'There's no other way. Those places are verminous, and we don't know enough about this disease to take any chances. For all we know, mice and bugs could act as hosts while remaining unaffected themselves.'

'Did Jelks tell you what he had discovered about the bacteria?'

'Yes.' Lanridge looked at the officer. 'What's on your mind, Sam?'

'I was just thinking. From what he told me the normal methods of fighting disease are useless. We can't vaccinate or immunise because the body has no antibiotics against the bacteria, and can't produce any. In that case, the only really effective counter-measure is isolation and sterilization.'

'That's about it,' said Lanridge evenly. 'Sounds simple, doesn't it?' He gestured towards the map. 'But in the city are twenty million people, most of whom are away from their homes. How long can you keep an entire city in house-quarantine? How can you control twenty million people when panic starts and they realise that they are living in a plague area?'

'I see what you mean,' said Sam. 'It isn't going to be pleasant.'

'It's going to be nowhere near pleasant,' said Lanridge grimly. 'But it's got to be done. The city is sealed and no one will get in or out until this thing is finally settled. With luck, we can beat it in,' he glanced at his watch, 'another thirty-three hours. With co-operation, that is. If people break quarantine and start moving around we'll have to start all over again.'

'Why so long? I thought twenty-four hours was the critical period?'

'I'm playing it safe,' explained Lanridge. 'The local quarantine broke down in twelve hours. It took time for the people to realise that the freeze-or-else order meant what it said. I want the city in stasis until all danger of contamination has passed. If we can enforce the order, we can do it. If we can't, then New York can be written off as a total loss.'

He didn't elaborate, and he didn't have to. Once the plague got out of control twenty million people would die. And if the quarantine order could not be maintained, then the disease would get out of control. Lanridge was obviously determined to see that his order was obeyed. He swore softly to himself as an unmarked patch on the map turned a vivid red.

'More trouble! That place should have been charted by the investigation teams.' He brushed past Sam on his way to a phone and the captain heard him give swift orders to the officer in charge of that area. He returned shaking his head. 'No co-operation,' he complained. 'The chances are that everyone we question is lying through fear, or desire to please, or just because we wear uniforms and give orders.' He stared at Sam as if seeing him for the first time. 'Well? How about getting down to work?'

'That's why I'm here.' Sam wasn't annoyed at the colonel's abruptness. Lanridge had enough responsibility on his shoulders without having to worry about trifles such as politeness. 'What do you want me to do?'

'Take over from Lessacre; he's out on his feet. Check the investigation teams and handle any emergency.'

Sam collected an orderly, relieved the officer and got down to work. 'Check section eleven,' he said to the girl. 'Find out if teams have visited the address of Joe Leghorn.' He repeated it twice to make sure she understood. 'He died of the disease; probably caught it from Johanasen. Check everyone living in his lodging house, and check his office, too, he may have gone there. Then try . . . '

Check this, check that, try everything and anything possible. Check the restaurant where he usually ate, the bars that he may have frequented, the public video-phones he may have used just before someone else. And not only for one man, but for everyone who was reported dead. Check back so as to try and find all he may have infected, so that the health teams could be on the spot. Check everything humanly possible, and then there still would be uncovered loopholes.

A sneeze could have infected a pedestrian. A cough the same. A Blue could have picked up a freshly discarded cigarette end. Someone could have accepted money from a perspiring hand. How to stop the invisible killer?

The answer: wait. Wait until it revealed itself in patches of flaring red on the map. Then send out the teams to seal the area. Send out more teams to check the probable path of the disease so as to try and get one jump ahead, to guess where the danger spots were.

And keep the people off the streets. Keep them pinned down so that, if one of them had the disease, it would remain localised. But the Health Army was limited. First priority was the red areas that had to be ringed with guards, the inhabitants sealed in cover-skins and then transported to a lazar house. Second priority was to the yellow areas in which the killer might strike at any time, and cause mindless panic. Again, these areas had to be ringed with guards. The rest of the city was covered by patrols and ruled by fear.

Three hundred people had been shot down before the populace realised that the freeze-or-else order meant exactly what it said. Two hundred more died as they broke quarantine and made a race for home and supposed safety. Fifty more had been killed for no other reason than that they thought it fun to run the patrol gauntlet. Now the people knew the guards meant business but, as the hours dragged past, tension began to mount.

It was no longer a joke. Men and women were hungry and tired, without cigarettes and faced with something they didn't have the mental equipment to handle. Hysteria began to blind them to the dangers outside.

'Sector nine,' droned a wall-speaker. 'Trouble at the corner of Plymouth and Vine. Breakout from a building by about two hundred people. Guards can't handle them.'

'Order copters three and six to bomb the area with tear gas,' ordered Sam. 'Send the section's reserves to the area. No shooting unless unavoidable, but use machine guns if necessary.'

'Sector nineteen.' Even the wall-speaker sounded tired. 'Car fifteen reports that missiles are being thrown from windows along Madison Avenue. Car thirteen wrecked and crew dead.'

'Order copter eleven to drift along the avenue and fire warning shots at all open windows.' Sam reached for a phone. 'Operator, get me the radio station, local services. Hurry!' He waited impatiently as the screen flashed with colour then revealed the image of a man. He was a young man wearing a lilac suit, and his smile was as artificial as the wave in his hair.

'Yes?'

'Captain Falkirk, World Police,' Sam identified himself. 'I want a message put out on all channels.'

'Another message!' The young man looked pained. 'But our schedule! You've already ruined it by your previous orders and . . . '

'Shut up and listen.' Sam was in no mood to bandy words with this simpering fool. 'This is a warning. All windows must be kept closed against copter-dropped gas. The gas is a fumigant with a high irritant quality and will tend to hover at the higher levels. Complete protection will be afforded against the effects of the gas if all windows are kept firmly closed. Now get that out immediately and repeat every five minutes for the next half hour.'

'I'll handle it.' The young man bit his nails. 'Is it as bad as they say?'

'Is what bad?'

'You know, the plague. Is it true that the streets are filled with dead?'

'Why don't you go outside and take a look?' Sam wondered who had spread the rumour, and just how far from reality it now was.

'Go outside?' The young man shuddered. 'Are you joking?'

'No. If you are worried, then go out into the streets and see for yourself.' Sam shrugged. 'Of course, you'll be shot if you do, but then you won't be worried any more, will you?' He cut the connection before the young man could answer, and discovered Lanridge standing beside him. The colonel held out a cup of coffee and a pack of cigarettes.

'Time you quit,' he said. 'Lessacre can take over from you now.'

'He's asleep.' Sam ripped open the package and lit a cigarette.

'He was asleep,' corrected Lanridge. 'You've been on duty longer than you think.'

'Have I?' Sam glanced at his watch, held it to his ear and wound it. 'How are we going now?'

'I think that we've got on top of it.' Lanridge gestured towards the map. The poorer sections were splotched with angry red. 'No new outbreaks for some time. We must wait another twelve hours at least before we can be sure.'

'And then?'

'Then we quarantine the infected areas and release the general freeze.'

'So soon?' Sam frowned. 'Wouldn't it be better to wait until the agreed period?'

'It would, but we can't do it.' Lanridge sounded very tired. 'Twenty million people need a lot of feeding, Sam, and no food is coming into the city. But that isn't the real reason. We simply cannot enforce the general freeze much longer. Incidents are piling up; another three cars

wrecked by missiles dropped from buildings, two outbreaks resulting in eighty dead
and injured, a fire . . . ' Lanridge swallowed. 'I don't like to think about that.'

'I see.' Sam didn't ask for details; he
didn't want to know. Lanridge fought disease as earlier soldiers had fought enemies
of flesh and blood, and now, as then,
casualties were to be expected. But Sam
was glad that he hadn't had to make the
decisions and accept the responsibility.

He rose and stepped towards the map,
his eyes tracing familiar streets. A patch of
red reminded him of Father Rosen. The
mission, naturally; infected Blues from
Johanasen's must have passed on the
disease. Lanridge came up beside him.

'That was a bad one,' he said quietly.
'We're using it as a dumping ground for
the dead.'

So they would all burn together, the
priest, the Blues, the drifters and loafers,
the respectable and the poor who had
fallen victim to the plague and who were
now, as never before, equal in the sight of
God and man.

'Go and have some rest,' ordered

Lanridge. He became stern. 'Get out of here. Go up to your office and bed down for a while. There's nothing else you can do here now.'

Sam was too tired to argue. He had been awake for almost sixty hours and had been through a strain when waiting to discover whether or not he was going to live or die. The elevator took him back upstairs and Mike blinked at him with bloodshot eyes as he entered the office.

'How's it going?'

'We're winning.' Sam slumped in his chair. 'You got any of those pills left?'

'Sorry, used the last a few hours ago.' Mike looked concerned. 'I'll send down for coffee though, maybe that'll help.'

'That and about a week's sleep.' Sam relaxed, feeling tiredness numb his limbs. 'Anything come up while I was down-stairs?'

'Not much.' Mike picked up a flimsy. 'This came in last night but I didn't think it worth bothering you with. Senator Rayburn's in a lazar house.'

Sam hadn't heard him; he was already asleep.

16

Nagati finds the Buddha

Rayburn wasn't worried by the general freeze. He had worries of his own. When a man took the longevity treatment there were three ways by which he could safeguard his future. He could buy residence in a Restezee Home where he would be taken care of to the extent of the interest on his money less certain charges. He could leave his money to his heirs and depend on their charity. He could convert all his holdings into cash, hide the money, and hope that none of the human wolves who took an interest in such things would track him down.

Worried or not, Rayburn didn't have much choice. He had no heirs, and so the usual solution was closed to him. For the first time he regretted his bachelor existence; a son, now, would have solved the problem. A young man ready and willing to be guided and advised by his father. An extension, in effect, of himself. But now it was too late for that. He could adopt an heir, true, but Rayburn had lived too long to put any trust in the generosity of strangers. Hiding his money was also out. Even if he managed to dodge the thieves, it was a barren solution. The legally dead could not open a bank account, own shares or safeguard their money in any way. Compound interest was something that no bank was willing to grant an immortal. He was left with the only remaining solution.

Irritably he riffled the colourful brochures scattered before him on his desk. They were all the same: each lauded the merits of a particular Restezee Home. All offered to end all worries about the future for a lump sum in cash or liquid assets to the same value. The Mariguana Home offered the freedom of a tropical island for a mere ten million dollars. The Holmanburg Home presented the joys of the Rockies for half that sum. A third, obviously aimed at a low-income group, promised bed and board coupled with healthy exercise for trifling five hundred thousand dollars.

Rayburn wasn't impressed. He'd seen some of the cheap Restezees. The beds were usually tiered bunks stacked in a barn, and privacy was non-existent. The board and exercise went together; you ate what you grew in a truck garden, or you didn't eat. He dropped the brochure, leaned back in his chair and stared at the ceiling.

It was very quiet, quieter than he had ever known it before. The freeze order had caught him at home alone and Rayburn wasn't used to being alone. Always, all his life, he had been surrounded by other people. As a boy he had shared a bed with three other children, worn hand-me-downs, eaten in rotation and learned to do his thinking in private. Even after he had cut away from the dead weight of family ties he had never known real solitude. Now, for the first time in his life, he was really alone.

He started as a car hummed past in the street outside, its turbine whining in tune with its tyres as it rounded a corner. For a moment he had hoped that it was Gerald returning, but it was only a patrol car prowling the streets. Restlessly, he rose and paced the room. He felt deflated, his ambitions seeming to have vanished in a cloud of depression. Probably it was because of his morbid study of the brochures. He hadn't sent for them, but they had arrived just the same. He was a public figure and his age was no secret. The promoting companies would have him on their files as a likely prospect.

Angrily he brushed them from is desk towards the wastepaper basket. They fluttered from the polished wood like a shower of coloured snowflakes, most of them falling on the carpet rather than in the basket. Rayburn glowered at them, half-inclined to leave them where they were; then, disturbed by the untidiness, stooped and picked them up. One pamphlet, different from the others, caught his eye and he straightened it with his hand.

It was from Prosper, and the cover showed a spaceship against a background of stars. It had been printed in luminous ink so that, as Rayburn held it beneath the desk light, it glowed with crawling colour. At any other time the senator would have thrown it wide, but now, from boredom, he began to read it. When he had finished he stared thoughtfully before him.

The pamphlet had been produced by experts, and both pictures and text had just the right balance of attention-catching appeal. For a man with nothing, it offered a new life; for a man with moderate wealth it offered far more than that. Venus, as Prosper pointed out, was not subject to Earth law. Any intelligent reader could guess what that meant, and Rayburn was far from being unintelligent.

The attention signal from the video-phone broke his reverie, the soft hum startlingly loud in the silence. He activated the screen. 'Yes?'

'Senator Rayburn?'

'Can't you recognise me?'

'Sorry, sir.' Mike's face on the screen betrayed his fatigue. 'This is just a routine call. Are you all right?'

'Certainly.'

'And your household? Of course, you

are alone.' Mike consulted something before him. 'We have located your aide. He is at Teterboro airport and is detained there for the duration of the emergency. He will be released as soon as possible.'

'And when will that be?' Rayburn did not make the mistake of trying to assert his authority to obtain quick release of his aide. He knew that, at the moment, he was only an individual in a city of individuals.

'That depends on Colonel Lanridge, sir.' Mike was pleasantly surprised that Rayburn had remained so calm.

'Naturally.' Rayburn hesitated. 'Any fresh news as to how this thing started?'

'No, sir.'

'There will, of course, be a full investigation?'

'I expect so, sir.' Mike was uncomfortable. He had a lot to do and didn't want to waste time. Yet to cut short the conversation would be rude. Rayburn solved the dilemma.

'Thank you, officer. Let me know if there are any new developments.'

Rayburn cut the connection and stared

thoughtfully at the blank screen. There would be an investigation, and he would see that he was in charge of it. The thing which had hit New York would horrify the nation, and if he could find the slightest scrap of proof tying it with the Orient he would turn the political situation upside down. But in the meantime . . .

He picked up Prosper's pamphlet and began to re-read it.

★   ★   ★

The freeze had caught Nagati in the house of Lang Ki, dealer in Oriental works of art. His presence was no accident. Sucamari hint to the dealers that he was interested in a certain type of art had brought results. When the dealer lad received the statue and box from Johanasen he had sent word to the Japanese legation of his new possession.

In this he was being both businesslike and careful. Such an item would be well known to a collector of Sucamari's standing, and, if it were stolen, he would learn from where and whom. In such a case he would enter into negotiations with the insurance company, taking a legitimate, if small reward. If, on the other hand, it was clean, then the Japanese would be the one most likely to offer a high figure.

Lang Ki, if he was disappointed that Sucamari could not honour him with his presence, did not show it. He ushered Nagati into his study, sent for tea, and embarked on a long and tedious session of Oriental pleasantries. Lang Ki had never seen the Orient, but that did not prevent him from acting the part of a gracious Mandarin. It was his means of asserting his individuality, and he erected around himself a fragment of culture that had died beneath the impact of modern civilization.

His study reflected his fantasy. Chinese tapestries hung against the walls and the low table was of teak inlaid with mother of pearl. Royal dragons writhed across scattered pieces of silk and everything was black lacquer and inlay. Nagati, though he had no patience with the dealer's make-believe, had no choice but to fit into the pattern. Not to have done so would have been to offend his host and, at all costs he must obtain the thing Lang Ki had for sale.

So he smiled and bowed as the dealer expanded before his audience. He spoke of a piece of jade he had recently acquired, depreciating it as unworthy and insisting that his guest study it to see how poor a thing it was. They drank endless tea in tiny cups so fragile that it seemed a breath would shatter the delicate porcelain. They chewed melon seeds and conversed in the singsong Cantonese which Nagati knew as well as his own language. Finally, Lang Ki got down to business.

The box was, he admitted, a pitiful thing and the statue it contained badly discoloured. Yet perhaps, it may have some interest for the gracious Sucamari. He rose and lifted the lid of a chest, pausing as a girl entered the room with the news of the general house quarantine. Philosophically, he shrugged, lifted the inlaid box from its resting place and set it on the low table.

'It seems that my poor house is to be honoured with your presence for many tranquil hours,' he said. 'All who are found on the streets will be shot. The girl has just brought the information. If you wish to make a call the videophone is at your disposal.'

'Thank you, but no.' Nagati had his own reasons for refusing. In time of emergency it was likely that private calls would be banned and, though he could possibly get through to Sucamari, the chances were that his call would be monitored. In any case, there might be a record of who he was and from where he was calling. Caution, now as never before, was of prime necessity. There was nothing to do but wait.

While they waited Lang Ki showed the aide the box. Carelessly he scratched the soft coating on the Buddha, using the same fingers to stuff more melon seeds into his mouth. Nagati dared not caution him, but it didn't matter. The dealer was as good as dead. Not just because he was handling the statue, but because disease was already loose in the city, and that disease had originated from what he held in his hands. Someone had become contaminated.

That someone had passed the box to a messenger and so passed on the disease. That messenger, in turn, had delivered it to Lang Ki, together with the box.

Nagati knew that he was in a house of the dying and that, he himself, was also a dying man.

He accepted the fact with the fatalism of the East, and immediately dismissed it for things of greater importance. If he should be found here with the box his death would implicate Sucamari and, through him, the Orient. The dreaded threat of retaliation would then be no longer merely a threat. He had to get away and take the box with him, and if possible deliver it to Sucamari. He, even now, could still carry out the plan if he possessed it and was free of suspicion.

Patiently he sat and toyed with the chessmen that Lang Ki had set on the table. He could afford to wait until almost dawn and then, whether Lang Ki was alive or not, he would have to make a break for it. If the dealer were still alive then Nagati would kill him.

The murder was unnecessary. Two hours before dawn the dealer hissed with pain, clutched at his chest and fell across the chessboard. Nagati wrapped up the parcel and headed for the door.

Outside, the streets shone with colour, the rain-wet concrete reflecting the gaudy advertisements. A patrol car hummed past, the light glinting from the barrels of rifles and light machine guns. Nagati shrank back into the doorway, waited until the street was clear, then darted forward along the sidewalk.

Luck favoured him, that and a shrewd and calculating mind. He ran at top speed down the streets then, as instinct and hearing warned him, dived into the shelter of doorways or side streets, standing motionless with his face to the wall and his hands hidden as the cars hummed past.

The tired men sitting in the cars were watching for movement, not oddly shaped shadows or patches of deeper darkness. Their eyes were burning with continual watching, their nerves tense with strain. They would have shot at anything that moved; but Nagati did not move. Unless he were trapped in a patch of light or ran when he should have halted, he stood a chance of reaching safety.

Circumstance dictated his route. He chose the darker streets and stayed away from the glittering shop fronts and so, inevitably, wended towards the poorer section of town. Here the cars were more frequent, their tyres whining as they raced around corners, their headlights and spotlights bathing the streets with brilliance.

Nagati froze as a car passed him, feeling his flesh cringe to an unexpected bullet. He turned and ran desperately towards an intersection, then skidded to a halt as sound and light signalled another car. He crossed the street, dived into an alley between two buildings and heard a shout as someone caught the hint of movement. Terror gave him strength and he ran faster, jumping over a glass-topped wall, not feeling the pain of his gashed hands. Before him a short passage gave onto an empty street and he raced towards it as turbines whined behind him and torchlight illuminated the wall over which he had jumped.

He reached the street and found that he had run into a trap. The block he was in formed the centre of a square, the alley being the only break in the row of houses. Within seconds cars would come from either end and the path behind him would be blocked. In a short while the guards would see him and their shots would follow at once.

There was only one thing left for him to do.

★ ★ ★

Rayburn started as he heard the frenzied pounding on the door. He was still awake, still fully dressed, despite the late hour. He had tried to sleep but the loneliness disturbed him. He had risen dressed, and now sat in the study glancing again at Prosper's pamphlet and toying with fantasies of himself as leader of a new world.

He rose as the pounding redoubled in violence and urgency. Above the noise he could hear the scream of tyres as they tore at concrete then the sharp, unmistakable sound of shots. Something whined through the air from the direction of the door and Rayburn stared at a jagged hole high in the panelling. Without thinking, he opened the door took a step forward and stared at what lay before him.

The man was Nagati, and he was dead. The aide had fallen on his back and his features were brilliantly illuminated by a spotlight from one of the cars halted outside the house. The same light also showed the pulpy redness of his chest and the opening where a bullet had torn its way from the body. Close to the dead man rested a small box of inlaid ivory.

'Don't touch that!'

Rayburn halted the motion of his arm and squinted towards the light. 'What's that?'

'Don't move!' A man stepped forward, his body huge against the light. He wore a heavy-duty cover-skin and carried a bundle in one hand. 'Catch!' He threw the bundle towards the senator. 'Go inside a little way, not too far, and leave the door open. Strip naked and put on that cover-skin. Hurry.'

'Why should I?' Rayburn remembered who and what he was. 'I am Senator Rayburn of the World Council and . . . '

'Shut your mouth and do as you're told!' Light glinted from the barrel of a rifle. 'I'm not arguing, mister. Personally, I'd rather not kill you, but I will if I have to.'

'You'd kill me?'

'You wouldn't be the first.' The man wasn't boasting, he was just stating a fact. 'I'm sorry about this, but it's your own fault. You shouldn't have opened the door. Now that you've been exposed we've no choice but to take you in and put you in close quarantine. Now, get that cover-skin on and don't waste any more time.'

Rayburn glanced once at the dead man, then began to undress with fingers which trembled on the zips and buttons. The air was dank and he shivered as he donned the plastic cover-skin, fumbling awkwardly with the seams and fastenings. It wasn't so much the cold that made him shiver as the sudden realisation that the guard had meant exactly what he'd said.

'What are you going to do with me?' Inside the garment his voice sounded too loud as it reflected back from the material. The answer, when it came, was muffled.

'You'll be taken to a lazar house. You've been exposed to the possibility of infection and you'll have to wear that suit for the next thirty hours. If you've got the disease you'll die. If you haven't, then you're safe as long as you don't open that coverskin. Understand?'

'I think so.' Rayburn restrained a desire to vomit. The sight of Nagati, dead and broken, had done something to his stomach. Death, in the abstract, was one thing, but something quite different when actually on the doorstep. To talk of eliminating potential enemies was merely to make sounds. To see them dead was something else. 'You'll inform the Council as to what has happened to me?'

'Sure. Senator Rayburn, you said?'

'That's right. And this man is Nagati, personal aide to Senator Sucamari.' He glanced at the box. Nagati must have been carrying it. 'Take care of that, it may be important.'

'We'll take care of it.' The guard hesitated. 'Sorry that I blew my top, senator, but it's been a hell of a night. I've never had to kill anyone before.'

'And I've never seen anyone die.' Rayburn looked again at the shattered chest and vacuous eyes of the dead man.

He had never had any strong feelings for Nagati. He had neither liked nor disliked him; not as he disliked Sucamari. He remembered how the aide had always seemed to be engrossed in a book; the sure sign of a lonely man. Books, to the lonely, are friends. Sometimes the only friends they have. Now Nagati had lost even those companions. But the bullet that had slammed into him had cost him more than a few books. It had cost him immortality.

Rayburn felt cold as he walked towards the waiting cars.

17

Death of a Samurai

Mike was sleeping when Jelks arrived at the office. He didn't wake until the doctor had shaken him, and then sat upright, rubbing his eyes.

'Doctor Jelks! I thought you were at the hospital.'

'I was.' Jelks rested a package on the desk. 'Where's Sam?'

'In the rest room getting some sleep.'

'Get him.' Jelks sat down as Mike left the office. Normally he would have joked with the secretary, but not now. Now he had no time or thought for anything but what he had discovered, and what had to be decided. He closed his burning eyes, then started, conscious that he had almost fallen asleep.

'You wanted me?' Sam sat heavily on a chair. He was haggard with fatigue.

'Yes.' Jelks fumbled for cigarettes and

couldn't find any. He'd been doing the same thing on and off for the past few hours, always forgetting to beg some after he had discovered that he was without. Mike saw the gesture, guessed what the doctor wanted and took a pack of his own from his desk.

'Here.'

'Thanks.' Jelks ripped open the package, annoyed at himself for the way his hands trembled. He was tired, yes, but he had been tired before. Fatigue shouldn't knot a man's stomach and fill his mouth with the taste of fear. He leaned forward as Mike offered a light and dragged smoke deep into his lungs. It tasted hot and acrid, something like burning feathers, but it stilled his craving. Or was it a craving? Maybe smoking was just a habit, a conditioned reflex similar to those Pavlov had discovered? He became aware that Sam was speaking.

'What did you want me for, Doc?'

'Private business.' Jelks glanced at the secretary. 'Send him outside.'

'What?' Mike was indignant. Sam cut short his objections.

'Leave us. See if you can hunt some coffee somewhere.' He waited until Mike had left. 'You had a reason for that?'

'A damn good reason.' Jelks reached for the package he had brought with him. 'This is for you alone, Sam. What you decide after what I'm going to tell you is up to you. I've spent hours trying figure it out and I can't do it.' He looked at the parcel. 'I've found the source of the disease.'

'You have!' Sam was interested. 'Tell me about it.'

'One of the patrols shot a man. He was trying to enter Rayburn's house when they got him, and he was carrying what's in that parcel. Rayburn came to the door at the wrong time and now he's in tight quarantine. Did you know that?'

'Mike had the report.' Sam wasn't interested in the senator. 'That isn't important.'

'No.' Jelks drew at his cigarette. 'Rayburn isn't important, but the man they shot is. The man was Nagati, and he was carrying this box.'

'This?' Sam unwrapped the parcel and

stared at the box. He ran his fingers over it until he found the hidden spring. The lid snapped open and he stared at the statue it contained. It shone with the peculiar lustre of polished ivory.

'It's clean,' said Jelks. 'I gave both it and the box the sonic and ultra violet treatment, and they couldn't hurt a baby. But when I received them the statue was coated with a nutrient culture for the new bacteria.'

'I see.' Sam closed the box, opened it again, then shut it with a snap. 'Nagati, you said?'

'Yes.' Jelks leaned forward. 'Are you thinking what I am, Sam?'

'Maybe.' Sam rested the box on the desk, then sat down and stared at it. He was a policeman and he was good at his job. Within his mind a jumble of pieces suddenly fell together to form a recognisable pattern. It all fitted, Augustine's death, the petty thief and the consequent outbreak of the disease. The summons for a messenger from the Japanese legation; a summons that they had denied. The missing girl and the Oriental nature of the box itself. Why Augustine had tampered with the parcel he didn't know, but that is not important. Neither was the irony that had made the statue of Buddha the carrier for the vile bacteria. The important thing was that he now knew who had tried to murder a city. Or had the main target been a nation? He grew conscious of Jelks staring at him.

'Why should Nagati have tried to deliver this thing to Rayburn?'

'Coincidence,' said Jelks. 'He was running the patrol gauntlet and they spotted him. He was terrified and tried to take cover. I doubt if he even knew just where was or who lived in the house.' He became thoughtful. 'Or maybe there's another reason. Rayburn doesn't like the Orient and isn't backward in saying so.'

'Assassination?' Sam considered it, then rejected it. 'No. The first reason is probably the correct one. Nagati wouldn't have wanted Rayburn to have discovered what was in this box. Can you imagine what would happen if Rayburn managed to tie what has happened here with the Orient?'

'That's why I'm here,' said Jelks simply. 'I didn't know what to do. Should I have destroyed it and forgotten what I discovered, or should I broadcast it? I just don't know, Sam. I'm a doctor, not a politician.'

'Neither am I,' reminded Sam. 'But you don't have to be a politician to guess what would happen if Rayburn found proof that the Orient was responsible for what has hit New York. He would accuse them of a plot to exterminate all human life in this hemisphere, and he could be right. But what happens then? Can we wipe out the Orient because of the work of a few fanatics? And if this was a national and not a private attempt, wouldn't they hit back?'

'Don't ask me.' Jelks made a helpless gesture. 'I can't handle it.'

'And you think I can?' Sam jerked to his feet and paced the floor. 'Damn it, Jelks, I'm only a captain in the World Police. I can't decide whether or not the world shall be plunged into war. It's outside my authority.'

'Passing the buck, Sam?'

'Aren't you?'

'Yes,' said Jelks slowly. 'I suppose that I am.' He looked down at his hands. 'I'm used to making decisions, I do it every time I operate, but this isn't like that. There's more than the life of one man at stake, and I don't have the facts on which to base a judgment. Is this an isolated incident? Is it the work of a few fanatics? Or is this just the prelude to a global war and the end of humanity? Can we dare to treat it as a local thing, or should we broadcast what we know?'

'To do that means war,' said Sam. He stared at the box. 'You've told no one else about this?'

'No.'

'Are you going to?'

'No, not unless you decide that I should.' Jelks shifted on his chair. 'What are you going to do, Sam?'

'There's only one thing I can do.' Sam wrapped the box and handed it to Jelks. 'Before we decide we must have the truth, all of it. Have you got anything which will make a man tell the truth, the whole truth and nothing but the truth?'

'I can get it. The medical room will have some.'

'Then get it and meet me downstairs.' Sam rose and headed towards the door. 'Hurry, Jelks, we've got a date at the Japanese Consulate.'

★   ★   ★

Sucamari sat alone in his Consulate tasting the bitterness of defeat and self-reproach. Everything had gone wrong from the moment when that fool of a girl had disobeyed his orders. The plan, so carefully conceived and carried out, had failed at the last moment. And the fault was his own. He had been guilty of excessive caution, forgetting, in his fear of retaliation, that great enterprises cannot be devoid of all risk.

He started at a pounding at the door, waited for a moment until he realised that all the servants were asleep, then hurried to the door with the vague hope that, somehow, Nagati had finally managed to return. The hope died as Sam and Jelks stepped forward. Behind them a patrol car, heavy with armed men, gave a touch of menace to the silent street.

'Gentlemen!' Sucamari smiled with automatic reflex. 'This is an honour.'

'Is it?' Sam brushed past the senator and entered the study. Jelks followed him, hugging the parcel in his arms. Sucamari glanced at it and felt a sudden fear. Despite that fear he was still smiling as he joined the others, closing the study door softly behind him. The smile annoyed Sam and, to cover his irritation, he stared at a solidiograph of Fujiyama, the model of the sacred mountain looking wonderfully realistic in the block of clear plastic. He turned as Jelks unwrapped the parcel.

'Do you recognise this box?'

'Should I?'

'I think you should,' said Sam. 'It is the contents of the parcel Augustine was delivering from someone in your legation. Nagati was carrying it.' He paused. 'We know all about it.'

'You talk in riddles, captain.' Sucamari clung desperately to the knowledge that, even now, there was no proof against him. No proof at all. They had the box and probably they had Nagati, but the aide would not talk. 'What is it that you say you know?'

'Open the box.' Sam pushed it across the desk towards the senator. 'Open it!'

'There is no need to shout.' Sucamari's fingers were clumsy as he fumbled with the box. He took a long time finding the spring and, when he pressed it, he stared for a long time at the statue.

'Your Devil's mixture has gone,' said Sam bitterly. 'But it has done enough damage. More than three thousand people have so far lost their lives because of it. You should be proud at what you have done.'

'I?' Sucamari lost his smile. 'Are you insane? Must I remind you who and what I am? How dare you infer that I am to blame for what has happened!'

'Stop it!' Sam fought the impulse to smash his fist against the other's mouth. 'This isn't a game we're playing. The time for verbal fencing is past. You know what happens next.' He nodded to Jelks and stepped towards the door.

'Wait!' Sucamari licked lips that had

suddenly grown dry. 'What are you going to do?'

'You are under arrest.' Sam was curt. 'You will be put on trial and, with the evidence I have against you, the verdict is predictable. You will probably be lobotomized and set to forced labour for the term of your natural life. I shouldn't have to tell you what the other repercussions will be; you know the political situation better than I do.'

'War,' said Sucamari. 'The frenzied terror of a nation of children who will seek to find safety in the destruction of humanity.' He stared down at the lining perfection of the Buddha, not seeing the age-old craftsmanship of the statue. It was over, finished, the great plan which had taken so much preparation and which could not be repeated. But though the plan was finished the incident was not. He looked at Sam. 'The Orient is innocent in this.'

'A nation is responsible for the actions of its representatives,' reminded Sam. 'But that is beside the point. The guilt of the Orient, or its innocence, can be

293

established at your trial.'

'No!' Sucamari felt perspiration ooze on his forehead. No matter what came out at the trial, the damage would be done. Rayburn would pounce like a hungry jackal and, innocent or not, the Orient would suffer. He, and the other Occidental representatives, would demand full retaliatory measures to be taken against the East. It was a thing that he had avoided, and the only way he could do that was by full and frank confession.

Sam heard him out, his face impassive.

'It is the truth,' Sucamari said. 'I swear it on my honour.'

'Honour?' Sam didn't smile, but it would have been better if he had. He looked at Jelks.

'All right, doctor, you know what to do.'

'I know.' Jelks took a hypogun from his pocket and stepped forward to face the senator. 'Bare your arm, please.'

'What is this?' Sucamari stared from the doctor to Sam and back to the doctor again. 'What are you going to do?'

'We are going to inject you with a drug

with a fancy name,' said Sam. 'Call it a truth serum and you will be as nearly correct as anything. It numbs the censor and opens the mind to questioning. You will feel no ill effects but, while beneath the influence of the drug, you will be unable to lie, retain information or be other than helpful.'

'I understand.' Sucamari bared his arm and watched as the doctor operated the hypogun. The high-pressured chemical penetrated the skin without pain, entering directly into the bloodstream.

Jelks glanced at his watch.

'Thirty seconds,' he said. 'Then talk.'

Sucamari talked.

He talked easily, fully, hiding nothing and wanting to hide nothing. He did more than just answer questions, he volunteered information, stripping his soul and confessing the motivations behind what he had done. He repeated what he had said before, but this time added details and his honesty was without question.

'What are you going to do, Sam?' Jelks had drawn the captain away from earshot of the senator. Sucamari sat and smiled at the solidiograph of Fujiyama. It was a genuine smile, not the artificial one he had cultivated so long, the smile of a man who has finally found inner peace by a complete dropping of his mental barricades.

'There's only one thing I can do,' said Sam. 'This isn't a national matter, but the work of fanatics. Yet if we take him to trial who will believe that?' Sam hesitated. 'He was telling the truth?'

'Of course. He was physically incapable of telling anything else.'

'I see.' Sam returned to the senator. 'This house is guarded,' he said. 'Set foot outside the door and you will be shot. It will be a regrettable accident, but you will be shot just the same.' He paused. 'Need I say more?'

'You are very explicit.' Sucamari drew a shuddering breath. He picked up the box, looked at the Buddha inside, then closed the box. 'It would please me if you took this. It is a rare piece and not without value, but take it for more than that. Accept it as a thank offering.'

'I will collect it on my return,' said Sam evenly. 'Shall we say two hours?'

'I understand.' Sucamari set down the box. 'One other thing. Nagati?'

'Dead.'

⋆　⋆　⋆

Sucamari stared at the closing door. A turbine whined in the street as the patrol car took Sam and Jelks back to the World Council buildings, the resulting silence seeming somehow more impressive than before. He had guessed that his aide was dead but it was still a shock to learn the truth. Nagati had been more than a servant to him; he had been almost a brother. Sucamari knew that he would miss him.

A small room opened from the study, a room with lacquered walls, hung with embroidered tapestries. A Shinto shrine stood at one end and a pair of Samurai swords hung against one wall. The place was heavy with the pungent scent of incense.

Sucamari undressed, stripping himself

297

naked before donning a robe of yellow silk. He took joss sticks from a cedar chest, lit them and set them before the shrine. He placed a soft cushion on the floor then, moving almost as if he were in a dream, he took down the swords from the wall.

There were two of them, one long the other short. Regretfully, he set the long one aside and, holding the other, slowly drew the blade from its lacquered scabbard. The steel was brightly polished and the soft light from the shrine flared from the razor-edge so that it looked feathery and unreal, the 'cloud-edge' which was the hallmark of the ancient craftsmen who had made the weapons of the warrior class.

Sucamari stared at it for a long time, letting his fingers caress the steel, his eyes blank and his face impassive. Kneeling on the cushion, he opened his robe so that the light gleamed on his yellow skin. Taking up the short sword he held it in both hands, the point aimed towards his stomach, his knuckles whitening as he gripped the hilt.

Now he missed Nagati. His friend should have stood by his side, the long sword naked in his hands, ready to strike the fatal blow should his courage fail. But Nagati was dead, and what he had to do he had to do alone.

Sucamari tensed himself, then drove the short sword deep into the pit of his stomach.

He was a long time dying.

18

New worlds

Three days after the end of the general quarantine New York had almost returned to normal. The substrips were moving again, the streets and sidewalks clogged with their usual traffic but, over the still-quarantined sections, thin columns of smoke rose towards the sky. The sterilization squads were still at work burning the dead and the condemned buildings. They would be reduced to ash, the sites would be cleared and new buildings would rear in their place, a permanent memorial to the horror that had struck and passed away.

Sam Falkirk stood at his office window and stared at the columns of smoke, then let his eyes drift over the jagged skyline of the city. Behind him the small sounds of office routine were suddenly broken. He turned as Jelks walked towards him.

'Well, Sam, it's all over.' Sleep and end of strain had restored the doctor's good humour. 'Lanridge tells me that another two days and we can forget the whole episode.'

'Can we?' Sam stared thoughtfully at the doctor. 'Tell me, when you treat a patient suffering from boils are you happy just to clear up the local infection or do you wonder why he got it in the first place?'

'I look for the cause of the trouble,' said Jelks immediately. 'Treating symptoms has been out of date for a long time. What made you mention boils? Have you any?'

'I haven't.' Sam gestured towards the city outside the window. 'But society has.'

'I know what you mean.' Jelks glanced to where Mike sat before the intercom. 'Let's go somewhere where we can talk.'

The visitors' gallery was closed, but Sam's uniform gained them entry. Jelks sat on one of the public benches and stared down into the assembly chamber where the minor officials of the Council were busy preparing for the day's business. A couple of newsfax reporters smoked as they tested their equipment.

'I heard about Sucamari,' said Jelks quietly. He looked at Sam. 'If he hadn't done it himself, would you . . . '

'I would.' Sam remembered what he had found when he had returned to the Consulate. 'Nasty way to die.'

'Hari-kiri?' Jelks nodded. 'I agree, but he didn't do it properly. The trick is to drag the blade sideways so as to effect a complete disembowelment. When that happens shock and loss of blood bring almost immediate death. Sucamari muffed the job; he should have had a friend to help him out.'

'Maybe.' Sam didn't want to talk about it. 'Did you cover your end?'

'Yes. I reported that the bacteria was a mutated strain of low survival factor and would probably not be repeated.'

'Is Lanridge going to believe that?'

'I hope so. I covered it with plenty of jargon and hinted that a leaking atomic generator could be the cause. Thin, but it's as good an excuse as any.' Jelks pursed his lips. 'It's probably true in part at that. That bacteria was not a normal culture. Sucamari was a little crazy, but cunning with it. If he'd managed to introduce the stuff into that beef extract as he planned we'd have been wiped out.' Jelks rubbed the fingers of his right hand over the back of his left. 'Did you . . . '

'I did. On paper, everything's clear. Augustine was the initial carrier, the parcel isn't mentioned, and Sucamari killed himself over grief for his friend. I even sent the box and statue to Rayburn. He'd seen it, remember, and I thought it best. He can test it any way he wants to, it won't tell him anything.' Sam shrugged. 'It was as unofficial as hell, but I cleared up the mess. It won't happen again until the next time.'

'The next time?'

'Sucamari's dead and his plot died with him,' said Sam. 'But the conditions which gave birth to his crazy idea haven't altered for anything but the worse. We were lucky in managing to stamp out this one infection, but does that eliminate the possibility that there will be others?'

'Like a man with boils,' said Jelks. 'You've got to hit at the root, not treat the symptoms.'

'That's about it,' said Sam. 'But how can you cure the disease without killing the patient? Society's sick, Jelks. We're not geared for longevity. We're not even geared to a machine civilization, and we've got both. Maybe we should just hand over to the Blues and let them run things. At least, they're mature.'

'No.' Jelks was serious. 'I won't deny that it's been talked about, and quite a lot of Blues are all for the idea. We could do it, you know, Sam. It wouldn't be hard to move in; a little bloody perhaps, but not hard. Not when half the population are Blues. But it wouldn't be the right way.'

'It may be the only way,' said Sam. 'Let the Blues work and support the youngsters. It makes sense.'

'It would lead to stasis.' Jelks produced cigarettes, offered them and lit his own. He smiled as he pocketed the package. 'Remind me to repay Mike for those cigarettes he gave me, I figure that I owe him at least a carton.'

'Keep to the point. Why would it lead to stasis?'

'For the same reason that the Chinese

culture remained static until the impact of Western ideology. The old aren't progressive, Sam; we have proof of that. In a hundred years prior to Blue we advanced from steam to atomic power. Since Blue we've done little. We've built a few houses, started a few sea farms, turned to hydroponics, but only because we had to. But we haven't made any real progress. Old men are conservative and are afraid to take chances. They don't like change and will fight against it. The Chinese were in stasis because of their ancestor worship; to improve the methods used by their fathers was tantamount to sacrilege. You can see the analogy.'

Sam could see it; it affected every sphere of life. The old did not die and so could not be forgotten. The Western nations had never been ancestor-worshippers, but they were rapidly becoming so. A man can't deny his own parents, grandparents and great-grandparents, not when they are around all the time. Orthodox religion, even though few practised it, had left its mark. The Fifth Commandment still had power. And it was all the more powerful because it was impossible to forget that, one day, every man and woman would become a Blue.

'Interstellar space flight could have saved us,' said Jelks, and Sam realised that the doctor was almost talking to himself. 'But when Shizzy Murphy died the oldsters got scared. They were still in control then and it took a lot of money to provide that tomb circling the Earth. They needed that money for other things, and perhaps they were right. But flight to the stars could have saved us.'

'It still can,' reminded Sam. 'Don't forget Prosper.'

'One man can't save a world.'

Jelks turned as the doors at the end of the gallery opened and a few visitors filed in. They were tourists from the Mid-West, and one of them, a farmer by his appearance, was talking to a friend. He didn't seem to think it necessary to lower his voice.

'I tell you I got it straight from Waterman. It's a fact.'

'Waterman ain't the Senator,' said the friend. He was plainly sceptical. 'What's

Rayburn want to back Prosper for anyway? How's that going to help us?'

'That's what we're here to find out. Now shut up and listen; he'll be on the floor in a minute.'

'Did you know about this?' Jelks looked at Sam, then down into the assembly chamber. 'Is Rayburn going to back Prosper's Alpha Project?'

'I don't know.' Sam was gently humorous. 'I've been busy lately, remember? But if Rayburn's really found himself another hobbyhorse, then I'm grateful. It'll take his mind off Sucamari and the Orient.' He fell silent as the assembly got down to business.

Outwardly Rayburn looked just as he had always done, the down-to-earth, plain-speaking farmer who knew the value of a dollar, and who wasn't going to be swindled in no horse-trade. But now he was quieter, more subdued, and he waited his turn to speak without any of the irritating gestures he had formerly used to attract attention to himself from the chair. Something had obviously happened to the Senator.

That something was thirty hours in a cover-skin waiting to die.

It was an experience that Rayburn would never forget. At first he had been numbed with the shock of Nagati's death, then, as the true horror of his situation had fully registered, he had gone a little mad.

The guards had taken him to a lazar house, thrust him in a room with a hundred others, warned him not to open his protective covering, then left him to pass the next thirty hours as best as he could. Those thirty hours had been a simple preview of Hell.

It was the uncertainty more than anything else, the not knowing if he was going to live or die. Rayburn had always feared death, and in that he was normal. No one now could be philosophical about something that need not happen. Death was no longer inevitable. Men fought to live, insisted on every safeguard against accidents which could cripple or maim, and regarded death in the same light that the early Christians had regarded Original Sin.

Men had died in the lazar house. There had been cursing and praying to a God which most had forgotten. There had been some fighting, and several had gone completely insane. And Rayburn had experienced a foretaste of war.

He had always advocated war; not in honest, outright terms, but in ambiguous phraseology. He had supported a programme that would have led to open hostilities and he had considered that programme justified. But it was one thing to talk of destroying an enemy and another to see that enemy spilling blood on your doorstep. One thing to laud the glories of combat, another to be the victim of combat.

Sitting in the lazar house, Rayburn had learned the meaning of fear. It was the fear that the entire world had once known, the nerve-sapping knowledge that he was just a unit among other units, and was defenceless to protect himself or to protest against the thing that had been done to him. He understood a little of the horror of war and, as the hours dragged past and his fear mounted, something happened to the Senator.

He became suddenly adult.

Adults, real adults, do not engage in the wanton waste of war. Mature people are constructive, not destructive, and, to the grown, life is a precious thing and not to be thrown aside for the sake of imagined insult, pride, the tap of a drum or the flutter of a pennant. Rayburn, when he left the lazar house, together with twenty survivors of the original hundred, was not the same man as when he went in.

'Incredible!' Jelks leaned back as Rayburn terminated his opening address. 'He means it. He really means it.'

'If you're surprised, then look at the others.' Sam gestured to where the news-fax reporters were sweating over their instruments. 'But why has he suddenly swung from Nationalism to an outright support of Prosper? I didn't know that Rayburn had the slightest interest in interstellar travel.' He rose to his feet. 'Let's find Waterman and get to the bottom of this.'

Gerald Waterman was in his Legation's

office. He had pleaded a headache and Rayburn, surprisingly considerate, had not insisted that he attend the assembly chamber. Not that it was necessary for him to attend at all; Gerald knew exactly what the Senator was going to say and how he had arranged his support. What worried him was what the Mariguana group would say when they learned that their dream of taking over a new world and using it as their private empire had burst like an over-ripe melon.

He straightened as Sam and Jelks entered the office; listened to what they had to say, then nodded. 'It's true, right enough,' he said gloomily. 'I don't know what happened to the Senator, but he sent for Prosper as soon as he was freed from quarantine and the two of them have had their heads together ever since.'

'Then he's sincere about this?' Jelks still couldn't believe it.

'He's sincere enough,' sighed Gerald. 'If you'd listened to half the propaganda I have, you couldn't doubt it.'

'Amazing!' Jelks looked at Sam and raised his eyebrows. 'Do you remember what I said about space flight providing the answer?'

'I remember.' Sam was thoughtful. He had the mental image of a growing weight crushing down on the world, a weight that had to be syphoned away — and quickly. But was Prosper the answer? Would his invention really work? Gerald had the answer to that.

'Rayburn's got it all worked out,' he said. 'Prosper swears that we can live on Alpha IV, so the Senator is going to set up a regular schedule to carry Blues to the new world. The cloud layer affords protection from the ultra-violet,' he explained, 'so the environment should prove ideal for albinos.'

'That's us,' said Jelks. 'But can he get the Council to agree to the project?'

'He can.' Gerald was very positive. 'He's already made deals with the other senators, especially those of the Asiatic Bloc. He's agreed to vote for the Calcutta project and others like it if they'll back his new motion. They will, of course; they'll only be too glad to get him out of their hair. And he'll have the farm vote of his own area firm behind him all the way. Those farmers will jump at the chance of free land, even if they can't get it until after they've taken the treatment and it's on another world.'

He wasn't happy about it. The Mariguana group had wanted Rayburn to support their new company, but only in order to use government money to save their own. But the Senator had literally taken over the project and Gerald could guess why.

Rayburn had to have a hobbyhorse and, now that he had turned from Nationalism, Prosper offered the perfect substitute. It was harmless, constructive and could provide what Rayburn wanted most of all — personal power after he had taken the treatment. He, too, had realised that, on Alpha IV, the old laws need not apply, and could not apply, if the immigrants were all Blues.

If the project succeeded he could remain in politics for centuries.

But the Mariguana group weren't going to like what had happened. They had been overbearing with Prosper, and it was natural that he should have deserted them for any other backer. They had underestimated Rayburn, he intended to be nobody's servant. They had bossed their own family for so long that they had forgotten that others would not recognise their power, but they wouldn't think of that. The blame would, inevitably, be placed on Gerald. He was too busy thinking about it to notice when Sam and Jelks left the office.

They halted by a window overlooking the city and stared at the sprawling mass of buildings below, each busy with his thoughts.

'It will work,' said Jelks positively. 'With Prosper's portal we can colonize other worlds. I know it.'

'Does age bring pre-vision?' Sam wasn't being ironic. 'How can you be so sure?'

'I'm sure,' said Jelks. 'The idea of the portal isn't new; we could have reached the stars fifty years ago if we'd really wanted to. Now we're going to reach them because we have to. Man is due to expand beyond the world of his birth,

Sam. And there's no telling where it will end.'

'A dream,' said Sam. 'Prosper's had it all his life. Why did he have to wait so long?'

'Because it wasn't time.' Jelks was serious. 'Things happen because they must, Sam, not because men want them to. The Greeks could have had steam power; they knew about it, but it remained a toy because it wasn't due to appear. We advanced from steam power to atomic energy in a single lifetime. Why? Was it because our fossil fuels were becoming exhausted? Or was it because atomic power is essential to reach the stars? Blue discovered his serum just as we had venture into space. Again coincidence?'

'What else? Are you trying to tell me that we are just pawns in a colossal game of chess? Or that all our achievements are the result of destiny?'

'I don't know.' Jelks shook his head. 'Maybe if I knew what makes the eel travel across the ocean from the Sargasso, or why lemmings migrate, I could give you an answer. They do what they do because they must.' He gave a short laugh. 'I'm not a religious man, Sam, but it's hard to dismiss the concept of a power greater than ourselves working with and by us. You know what's going to happen, don't you? All the old legends and promises will come true. Men are going to die and then go to another world. It will be legal death, and the other world will be Alpha IV, but that makes no difference. And after Alpha and Proxima Centauri will come other stars with their infinity of worlds. Enough worlds and enough space to take care of all the immortals there could ever be. The old will go, Sam, and the young, the meek, will inherit the Earth.'

It was true, and Sam knew it. What Jelks had said would happen: because it must. Mankind had to expand. Long life demanded a wide stage on which to act itself out. Immortality demanded nothing less than the universe.

So Prosper's portal would bear away from the mother world those men and women who had reached maturity. An adult in a playpen is a nuisance, a dead weight on the imagination and development of the children. A stultifying influence, respected but unwanted. But, equally so, children could not be at home among the stars. So Earth would remain the cradle of the race, but the universe would supply the room in which the adults could move.

Sam drew a deep breath, feeling sudden, tremendous lightening of his heart. But he was not thinking of the distant future for the destiny that men, all unknowing, were working out. He was thinking of more immediate things. He was thinking of Carmen, and marriage, and the children he was no longer afraid to have.

THE END

We do hope that you have enjoyed reading this large print book.

Did you know that all of our titles are available for purchase?

We publish a wide range of high quality large print books including:
Romances, Mysteries, Classics
General Fiction
Non Fiction and Westerns

Special interest titles available in large print are:
The Little Oxford Dictionary
Music Book, Song Book
Hymn Book, Service Book

Also available from us courtesy of Oxford University Press:
Young Readers' Dictionary
(large print edition)
Young Readers' Thesaurus
(large print edition)

For further information or a free brochure, please contact us at:
Ulverscroft Large Print Books Ltd.,
The Green, Bradgate Road, Anstey,
Leicester, LE7 7FU, England.
Tel: (00 44) **0116 236 4325**
Fax: (00 44) **0116 234 0205**

Visiting Galloway's flat in London, Inspector Merritt had an outrageous proposition to offer him: he was to go to America to steal paintings originally stolen from London's Bedford Art Gallery. Galloway could keep the huge amount of money involved, providing he could re-steal the paintings, outsmart the American police and the gangsters who had the paintings, get that money, and return to London. He accepts the challenge and manages to succeed — but not before some uncomfortably close calls.

THE HURRICANE DRIFT

John Newton Chance

Jonathan Blake was an adventurer on holiday and when the hurricane came he flew from it, taking a woman called Jo with him. But the hurricane, and the wrath of the lady's husband, follows them . . . Landing on a secret island proves to be a dangerous move, leaving Blake wondering whether to fight 'em or join 'em. When he does both, it seems that calamity is inevitable. But perhaps there is a way of escape after all . . .

A COPPER SNARE

Lawrence Williams

Meet Detective Constable 'Randy' Jack Bull. Despite his nickname he is not happy with all the women in his life. Some of them are untrustworthy, some are mad — and some are dead. He also discovers that, as he watches his women, other people are watching him. Becoming increasingly bewildered by the case he is working on, and exhausted by overwork, he is all too easily ensnared by the melodramatic events that follow Carnival Night . . .

WHAT HAPPENED TO HAMMOND?

John Russell Fearn

How could a dead body travel sixty miles almost instantaneously through a bitter winter's night? Chief Inspector Garth could deal with three-dimensional problems, but Hammond's inexplicable transition was beyond him. Garth called in Dr. Carruthers to see if the eminent physicist could explain the mystery. The Doctor could! But not until a further baffling murder had been committed could Carruthers demonstrate — by means of a strangely airborne teapot — exactly what happened to Hammond.